Illusion of Love
by Nana Malone

With a deep inhale, she said, "Well, good night, Bennett. Tonight was fun."

His gaze dropped to her lips. "It was."

"I'll see you tomorrow for the photos if you're still interested."

"Oh, I'm interested."

Val wished she had more time to mentally brace herself, but when Bennett leaned close she couldn't move. Not a millimeter. All she wanted was his lips on hers, making her feel alive. Like the ride on his bike.

When he stepped close to her body, his whisper was low, harsh. "I have been dying to do this since you opened the door tonight."

From My Heart
by Sienna Mynx

"I guess this is good night," she said. "Thanks again."

She rose on her toes to kiss his cheek but her gesture was off by a fraction of an inch, bringing her mouth to the corner of his. Niccolo wasn't sure what came over him, but it happened with lightning-like speed. He turned his face and he kissed her. She gasped and went into his arms, opening her mouth fully to him. He brought an arm around her. Lust was rising up so hard and fast he was unable to keep it down.

Nana Malone is a *USA TODAY* bestselling author. Her love of all things romance and adventure started with a tattered romantic suspense she borrowed from her cousin on a sultry summer afternoon in Ghana at a precocious thirteen. She's been in love with kick-butt heroines ever since. You'll find Nana working hard on additional books for her series. And if she's not working or hiding in the closet reading, she's acting out scenes for her husband, daughter and puppy in sunny San Diego.

Books by Nana Malone

Harlequin Kimani Romance

Wrapped in Red with Sherelle Green
Tonight with Sienna Mynx
A Vow of Seduction with Jamie Pope
Unwrapping the Holidays with Sheryl Lister
This Is Love with Sienna Mynx

Sienna Mynx writes contemporary and historical multicultural romance. Her dramatic tales of forbidden love are for readers who love bad boys and desire to be the one to tame them. Sienna currently has thirty-four published books both as an indie author and with Harlequin Kimani Romance.

To learn more about future releases and projects currently underway, please visit The Diva's Pen, thedivaspen.com.

Books by Sienna Mynx

Harlequin Kimani Romance

Tonight with Nana Malone
This Is Love with Nana Malone

NANA MALONE
SIENNA MYNX

This is Love

HARLEQUIN® KIMANI™ ROMANCE

ISBN-13: 978-0-373-86485-0

This Is Love

Copyright © 2017 by Harlequin Books S.A.

The publisher acknowledges the copyright holders of the individual works as follows:

Illusion of Love
Copyright © 2017 by Nana Malone

From My Heart
Copyright © 2017 by Sienna Mynx

Recycling programs for this product may not exist in your area.

For questions and comments about the quality of this book please contact us at CustomerService@Harlequin.com.

HARLEQUIN®
www.Harlequin.com

Printed in U.S.A.

CONTENTS

To Erik, I love you. You know why.

Dear Reader,

Thank you so much for reading *Illusion of Love*. Anyone who knows me will tell you that I am Type A to the max! I love rules, plans and schedules. In *Illusion of Love*, I can feel Val's pain when she meets her complete opposite, Bennett. He frustrates her and pushes her to step out of the box. As someone who married her total opposite, I'll tell you, it makes for a fun adventure.

Next up for me—more books, including more Kimani Romances. So sit back, relax and happy reading!

If you want to chat with me, I'm pretty easy to find!

Nana Malone

www.nanamalone.com
www.Facebook.com/nanamalonewriter
www.Twitter.com/nanamalone

ILLUSION OF LOVE

Nana Malone

Chapter 1

Something was very wrong.

Valentine Anderson shifted in her oh-so-pretty Louboutins as she stared at her boyfriend. He was gesturing nervously and talking. Almost babbling. But try as she might to concentrate, all she heard was a monotone drone. *Focus, Val.* She forced her ears to pay attention.

"Here's the thing. I think you're great… I wasn't really looking for a relationship…you're fantastic…it's not you, it's me… I really care about you, but I need to find myself."

The find myself excuse was her personal favorite. Because it invited her to all those ragey places deep inside, where she never allowed herself to go. But then this was the third time she was being dumped on or just before Valentine's Day. She was allowed to get a little furious… right? Especially because this time she *needed* a boyfriend on Valentine's Day.

If she had time to analyze, she'd examine all the possible reasons why her last two boyfriends had dumped her when everything was seemingly fine.

First, there'd been Alejandro. Brazilian. Beautiful, with all that tanned skin and a brilliant smile. He'd claimed that they were getting too serious. He was the first finder of self.

Then there was Tyrell, though, really, she should have known better than to date a professional athlete. Tyrell was a beautiful man. All dark chocolate skin, combined with a wicked smile that was a pure invitation to sin. And sin he had…with her neighbor, and her hairstylist…and her masseuse.

And now James. It was three weeks to go before her sister's wedding on V Day and here she was hearing all the usual excuses.

"Like I said, I think you're great. You're just a bit… rigid for me."

Her brows snapped down. *Say what now?* "Rigid?"

He nodded enthusiastically, as if thrilled that she seemed to understand. "Yeah, I mean, you're a food blogger, so I thought you'd be more adventurous. In and out of bed. I thought we'd do more things and travel more, but you're really set in your routine."

Relax your jaw, Val. You keep clenching like this and you're going to crack a molar…again. "So you're breaking up with me because I didn't drop my life at a moment's notice to go to Montreal with you."

His eyes widened, as if he suddenly realized this would not be the calm breakup he'd anticipated. "No. Of course not. It's everything, really." He held up his hands. "I mean, obviously, we have chemistry. We do, but I need someone who's more fluid with life and open to ideas. You don't need me. Hell, you certainly don't *want* my opinion…"

As he talked, her mind raced. Yes, it sucked to be dumped. And even more it sucked to be dumped by someone like James. At the end of the day, she'd liked him, but she knew they weren't going to be a super long-term thing. But he was nice—at least she'd thought he was. But boy, oh, boy, the man whined. *A lot.*

But he'd been good enough to hang out with and at the very least show up at her sister's wedding with.

Her sister, Solstice, was getting married in a matter of weeks, and Val knew better than to show up to that wedding alone. No way was she going to yet another family function on her own. To have to endure her mother and aunties and sister bemoaning how she could possibly still be single was a special kind of torture. On her own… unloved. Never mind that she'd tried a million times to tell them that she wasn't lonely. That she had a perfectly full life with her job and her friends.

But the women in her family were old-school. Not even old-school as much as they defined how happy they could be in life only by what man loved them at the moment. Oh, and God forbid it was the wrong kind of man. Then everyone in the family would descend on him like a pack of vultures, leaving nothing left but a carcass.

James was supposed to be her avoid-criticism card. But now it was go directly to singledom hell. Do not pass Go. Do not collect $200.

The elevator dinged as James stumbled through his breakup speech, and all she wanted to do was climb into her bed and forget the whole night. That was until she caught sight of her neighbor Bennett Cooper strolling down the hall with a gorgeous brunette in tow.

Cue the grinding teeth again. The guy was the definition of bad neighbor. Loud music. A revolving door of women. Parties that went on all night. He had zero respect.

He also made her edgy. The constant awareness, making the hairs on the back of her neck stand up, was almost uncomfortable to bear whenever he was around. Every time he was near, she sat on razor's edge. Val was not a fan.

Maybe it was the way his intense green eyes tracked her, or the tattoos over his tanned flesh and whipcord-lean body with ridiculously defined muscles…if you liked that sort of thing. Her libido sat up and strutted. As if to say, *Hello, I like that sort of thing.*

There was no way she was going to be humiliated in front of him. She turned to rush James along. "James, if you're dropping me, say the words and get it over with. I have things to do."

Bennett Cooper needed a way out. How the hell had he ended up in this position?

When he'd agreed to a contract with publishing magnate Milton Voss, he'd been thinking of all the ways it would boost his career. Bennett might have the perfect dream job of photographing models, but he wanted more, and Voss could give it to him. For the last week, Bennett had been thinking about all the places he would travel. He'd been thinking this job meant the opportunity to make his father proud. He *hadn't* been thinking about Voss's wife. The same wife who had made a pass at him at his gallery opening last year. He'd managed to extricate himself from that situation, but *tonight*—tonight was a whole other ball game.

You have options, Ben. He could quit. But that wasn't in his nature. And he didn't run from a fight. *Except from the unpleasant memories from your past.* Damn, he really didn't need a subconscious battle right now. He needed an escape route.

Grabbing a drink downstairs with the creative director of Voss Magazines had been a good idea. The two of them saw eye to eye on a few things. While Voss owned the usual smatterings of sports magazines and women's magazines, the real passion in the company was nature conservation. Those were the kind of photos that would challenge Bennett and save the world. The kind of photos his father had taken. Game changers.

Not that he was opposed to fashion photography. Fashion came with models. And, well, models…enough said. But he'd always wanted to do more. *Be* more.

For years, his career had been growing steadily. Luckily he'd been able to avoid too many years as an assistant. At the point that his own street photographs with models he'd taken for free started to outshine those of his paid mentors, his phone had begun to ring off the hook. He'd never thought the scared, orphaned kid from Cali would ever have to say no to too much love. Except he had. But now everything was in jeopardy because Adriana Voss thought she had the hots for him.

His meeting with Stephen had wrapped up and he'd stayed to finish his drink. Next thing he knew, Adriana turned up, looking to see his latest pieces. He wasn't an idiot. He knew a setup when he saw one. She'd fooled Stephen into inviting her along or she'd checked his schedule. Either way it spelled bad news for Bennett.

The moment she wound her arm around his waist and lifted his drink before pressing it to her lips, he'd known he was in trouble. All kinds of trouble. Not that Adriana wasn't beautiful. She was. Even though she was pushing forty at least, she was stunning. With curves to give a man fantasies and a face that could easily have launched a thousand ships, she was the kind of woman that Bennett would happily have slept with. *If* she wasn't married.

That was a deal breaker for him. Yes, he was a womanizer. He loved women. A variety of women. And they were plentiful and available. But he didn't do married women. Not just for the headache, but also because, well, wrong. Second, he liked his boss. Genuinely liked the man, so he wasn't going there. But he had to be careful, because Adriana was well-known for her...vindictive streak.

"Benny, I can't wait to see your latest work. I mean, I made poor Milton buy every single photograph that wasn't already nailed down at your gallery the last time."

He swallowed hard. "It's Bennett, actually. Either Bennett or Ben." Benny had been his mother's nickname for him. It hurt to hear it.

"Okay, Bennett it is, then. Do you still have some of those self nudes you took?"

This was not his lucky day. The self nudes weren't really nudes. Just an illusion as he'd paid respect to one of his favorite artists. They stepped onto the elevator and he tried to think fast. He could pretend to get a call. He could call his best friend, Trevor, over. He could feign a tapeworm. *Something*...anything. Because no matter what he did, he would lose his job. But that wasn't going to happen. He wouldn't let it.

Adriana clung to his arm and he sighed. *Think. Think. You can do this, Bennett.* And then he saw it, his salvation. His prickly-as-hell neighbor. The two of them were *not* friends. Like, at all. Hell, they weren't even friendly. She was uptight and bossy, and a pain in his ass. She was always asking the co-op board to stop him from having parties.

His place was a work and live loft, just like hers. He couldn't help it if his lifestyle was more fun. He wasn't sure what it was she did for a living, but he knew she was tense. Like she had a stick jammed so far up her... Well, he'd just leave it at that. And she was with that needle-necked douche waffle she called a boyfriend.

Bennett was not a fan. Especially as the guy had hit on one of the models who left his place after a New Year's Eve shoot. He doubted Miss Prim and Proper knew about that. God, what he wouldn't give to rumple her up just a little. She'd probably never even dated a guy like him before, someone with edge, who didn't buy his clothes from the Nerds 'r' Us line. She had a type, and Bennett knew *he* wasn't it. But for tonight, maybe he could be.

Because right about now, it looked like Needle Neck was dumping her. What? Was that the second guy on or around Valentine's Day? The guy was dragging it out. Rookie mistake. When Bennett heard her say, "Can we get this show on the road?" it solidified his plan. He just prayed she didn't knee him in the balls.

Though given the alternative, he didn't really have much choice. "Ah, Adriana, look, you get to meet my girlfriend."

Voss's wife blinked up at him as if she was trying to compute the words. "G-girlfriend? I was told you were single."

He shook his head. "Not sure who told you that. But that's my girl, Valentine."

Adriana's brows drew up. "What kind of name is Valentine?"

Easy does it, mean girl. "It's the one her parents gave her." Carlton Banks twin was winding down, so Bennett only had a second to make this work if he was going to do it. He extricated himself from Adriana's astonishingly tight grasp. And strode right for Valentine. Her dark eyes widened as she watched him in surprise.

Easy on the family jewels, sweetheart. "Hi, baby. I see you're finally having that talk with John."

Pencil Pusher's brows rose. "It's James, actually."

Bennett shrugged. "Whatever."

Valentine stared at him, full lips parted and dark eyes wide. Bennett deliberately nudged James aside and went for it. *Go big or go broke, right?* He wound an arm around her waist, his mind briefly registering that she smelled like honeysuckle. And that she looked surprisingly sexy in her flared pink dress. But he didn't have time to drink in the image. He had a career to save.

Her soft gasp of shock was all he cataloged as he dipped his head and brushed his lips against hers. On first contact, his mind went blank. Completely absent of thought as joules of electricity shot through him, and he was forced to go on instinct.

She could have shoved at him, she could have kneed him in the nuts, and she could have slapped him. But Valentine Anderson did none of those things. What she did was make this sexy little mewling sound in the back of her throat, and Bennett lost his mind.

With that sound, she completely erased the present for him. No longer were they in the hallway with an audience, but they were alone, wrapped in a cocoon of just the two of them. Muttering a groan, he tested and delved his tongue inside her parted lips, and she responded by welcoming him with a slide of her own tongue.

She tasted sweet and hot, and so damn decadent that he automatically slid his hands down her back to tuck her against him.

But then something intruded into their space. Into their little safe haven. It wasn't her. Her nails dug into his shirt pulling him closer. And hell if he didn't *want* to be closer. He'd explore that little tidbit later.

There were words. Not his, not hers, other people's. Then the fog started to lift from his brain. Right. Carlton's twin and…oh, yeah, Adriana. He didn't want to stop kissing her, though. But he wanted to do it when they had more time, because just kissing her was enough to set his whole body on fire.

"Excuse me, Bennett."

Tearing his lips from Valentine's, he dragged his eyes open. He acknowledged Adriana's clipped words, but he couldn't look away from the neighbor, who up until now he'd always thought of her as the Pain in the Ass. "Yeah, Adriana?"

"Are we going to look at the artwork?"

Artwork? Artwork? What? Oh, yeah. He turned slowly. "Do you mind if I bring them by Voss later this week? I didn't realize Valentine was going to be home, and with our schedules—I know you understand." *More like no way in hell are you coming into my apartment.*

She narrowed her eyes at Valentine and tipped up her chin. "Fine. We'll talk later."

"Sure thing," Bennett said. He held his breath until the elevator doors closed on Adriana. Then he turned his attention back to James. "You're still here?"

James's mouth hung open, and Valentine stared. Bennett just kept his arm tucked around Valentine's waist. She didn't move away, nor did she say anything.

"Y-you two are together?" James asked.

Bennett held his breath. What was she going to say? Would she go along with the charade?

When she started to speak, her voice was deeper, huskier. "Yeah, James. This is actually why I wanted to go to dinner tonight. When you started to break up with me, I figured I'd let you take the out. This obviously isn't working. And Bennett and I are a…" Her voice trailed off as she cleared her throat. "…a thing."

Bennett bit the inside of his cheek to keep from laughing. Sure. *Thing* worked. "Hit the skids, James." The guy looked like he was going to argue, but then Bennett tucked her against his side more firmly. How had he never noticed how sexy she was? She was petite, but her body was a dream. And her soft breasts pressed into his side were a hell of a distraction.

James scowled and rolled his eyes, but with a muttered epithet or two under his breath, he headed down the hall for the elevator as well.

The moment the guy was out of earshot, the two of them jumped apart and Valentine rounded on him. "What the hell do you think you are doing?"

"Are you kidding me right now? I just saved you face. No humiliating breakup. Or do you mean to tell me that you wanted that sweater vest–wearing asswipe to dump you?"

"Where do you get off?" she muttered through clenched teeth.

It wasn't his fault. Honestly, it wasn't. But his lips twitched. He sometimes had the humor of a twelve-year-old boy. "Isn't that kind of a personal question, considering we just had our first kiss? But if you must know, the sho—"

Her eyes widened to saucers, and she covered her ears. "Oh. My. God. Do *not* share. You know what, from now on, you keep you and your thoughts to yourself."

Bennett grinned at her. "Come on, admit it. That was the hottest kiss you've had in months, if ever." Valentine's mouth hung open as she blinked at him. Once, then again.

Then she snapped her mouth shut, stepped back into her apartment and slammed the door in his face.

Oh, yeah, that went well.

Chapter 2

Bennett Cooper was an arrogant, inconsiderate, rude jerk. He had women in his place all the time, and besides his music, sometimes she could hear…his other activities. Not that she was listening.

Her loft unit and Bennett's were both on the south side of the building, and they both had wraparound decks that met in the middle. She faced the southwest and he the southeast, and both of them had a stunning view of lower Manhattan. She'd picked this building because it had a doorman, and it was exclusive.

Her foodie app and lifestyle brand had taken off two years ago, and her blog had blown up. Unfortunately that meant unwanted attention, making the doorman a necessity. But instead of exclusivity, she'd ended up with a neighbor from hell.

Val leaned against her door, too afraid to look through the peephole to see if he was still out there. Just the thought was enough to make butterflies dance low in her belly.

Slipping her feet out of the three-inch stunners, she slid her back against the door until she landed on her butt with a soft plop.

Touching her lips tentatively, she went over every distinct flavor and smell of him. The reason she was so good at what she did, the reason her blog and her brand were so popular, was her superior sense of smell and ability to taste all the ingredients and ferret out specific scents. Though her innate ability made her an anomaly, it also made her excellent at her job, and in a controlled environment her hyperosmia didn't get in the way of her normal life. For the most part.

Growing up had been difficult, though. Every smell assaulting her everywhere she went. And if someone couldn't cook, God help her. She could practically taste where things went wrong just from the aroma alone. And the bummer of it was she *loved* food. From burgers and cheesesteaks to filet mignon. But it had to be flavorful and it had to be good, or she couldn't eat it.

Her current problem was, while she loathed Bennett I'm the Neighbor from Hell Cooper, the man smelled *good*. Like better than good. Like steal one of his T-shirts and tuck it under her pillow good. In a totally nonstalkery way. He smelled of sandalwood and musk. And that odor set her every nerve ending on high alert in a good way. The scent of him still clung to her, and she just wanted to hug it to her and breathe deep.

Yes, she had problems. The other issue was the man tasted incredible. Tonight he'd had scotch. The good stuff. Something smoky and divine. He also tasted a little like mint. Not the kind that had so much sugar added that it obscured the taste of the actual mint. And there was something else there. Something sweet and delicious that she could eat all damn day, with one of those tiny dessert spoons where one bite was so decadent and delicious, you had to savor every bite. Yes, that was how he tasted.

And that was why this was trouble. Because he was the devil. With too much charm and far too much arrogance. And also because she'd never be able to look at him again without thinking about how good he tasted. Like she needed that headache.

And then, of course, there was James. Bennett Cooper kissing her had had one and only one upside…that she was willing to acknowledge, anyway. James hadn't been able to break up with her properly. She'd been the one to dump him. By way of a kiss. It was juvenile, but it felt good. To not have to hear the implication *You're not good enough for me. I want someone better.* Bennett Cooper and his wicked tongue had put her on top. *Wouldn't you love to be on top of him?*

Oh. My. God. This was bad. Terrible. She didn't want him. But now her body had Bennett on the libido and it wasn't going away. This called for reinforcements.

Dragging out her phone, she video dialed her best friend and started talking as soon as Mel answered. "James tried to dump me and the aggravating neighbor boy kissed me."

Her best friend waited two whole beats before speaking. "Honey, let me pop some popcorn, then you need to start from the beginning.

The popping popcorn was just a metaphor, so Val launched into the retelling of the second half of her night, down to the tongue teasing from Bennett-you-have-no-business-thinking-about-that-man-naked, sliding his tongue in between her lips and making her forget her name.

When she was done, Mel sat back on her couch. "Okay, first of all, I want that kiss story one more time at a later date, because that is the hottest thing I have ever heard. Second, good riddance on James."

"Good riddance? Are you forgetting that I need a date in three weeks? I can't show up alone *again*. I can't take it. And it's Sol's wedding. I can't skip it. But I am not making the trek to Princeton to have my whole family shake their head about how I cannot keep a man."

"Okay, good point there, but maybe since hot neighbor boy kissed you, you can take him."

Val stared at her friend. "I think you've lost your mind."

Mel held up her hand. "Hear me out. You keep dating these versions of he who shall not be named." Marcus, her ex from college. He'd been the perfect guy. Entrepreneur, good-looking. He'd done the whole Jack and Jill cotillion thing. Her parents loved him. But he'd broken up with her just before graduation, because he had political aspirations and he didn't think she fit the bill of a politician's wife. She'd been devastated, of course. And her family had blamed her.

"I do not," Val muttered.

"Let the record show, Alejandro and Tyrell and now James. All essentially carbon copies of each other. Stop trying to re-create the past. I mean, did you even like James?"

"Of course I liked James."

Mel raised a brow. "Oh, yeah? What did he taste like?"

Only Mel understood how Val categorized the men she dated. "I—"

"Go on, I'm waiting."

Val sighed. "He tasted like store-brand chocolate. Bland, overly sweetened and waxy."

"See? Who wants to kiss waxy for the rest of their life? And come on, you couldn't even bring yourself to sleep with the guy."

Val's mouth hung open. "Oh, my God. Would you stop?"

"Or did you mange that and somehow forget to tell me?"

"Okay, fine. But we were taking it slow."

"Yeah, yeah," Mel rolled her dark eyes. "So slow you were avoiding sleeping with him. Come on. You should have been done with him in the first week. Him and those sweater vests? He wasn't even hip enough to pull off that common look. You kept him because you figured it would be better to go home with someone than alone."

There were times in her life that she hated it when Mel was right. Times like this. "So, what, you suggest I find the nearest guy with a motorcycle, then ask for a ride?"

Mel howled with laughter. "Depends. Does hot neighbor ride a motorcycle?"

Val groaned. Come to think of it, he did have one. But she only ever noticed it in the summertime, when he brought it out of storage. "Yes, but that's hardly the point. Come on, I need a solution for the wedding."

"Okay, I'll come by tomorrow, and we'll go over all your options. Make you a fancy pro/con list for each available option and we'll fix this."

Val hung up with Mel and laid her head back against the door. Absently she played her fingertips along her lips. They still tingled from the remembered kiss, and her body was still far too warm for her liking.

Bennett Cooper wasn't on the list of potentials. Bad boy was so not her thing. It didn't matter how well he could kiss.

Chapter 3

Bennett had taken a calculated risk, and right about now he was sure that Adriana Voss was ready to kill him. Or have him fired...or jump his bones. He wasn't sure which. But none of those options worked for him. This job didn't just mean he'd get to shoot wildlife. It opened up his whole career. Voss owned more than just the magazine company. His name was all over galleries, museums and documentary exhibitions.

As promised, he'd taken the portfolio in to Voss Magazines' main offices. Even though her title was basically an empty one, as VP of styling or something like that, Adriana still had an office and still showed up to work. Apparently, Voss wanted his wife close to keep an eye on her.

When Bennett asked her assistant to see her, Adriana had come out with a saccharine smile and a suit that said *nothing about this is work appropriate*. It was one of those couture thingies that looked good on a model walking down the runway, but in real life, on a woman with curves, it was too low cut and too tight for the office.

But he'd gone in with a smile. "I'm so sorry we didn't get a chance to go over these the other day, but Val and I hadn't seen each other in a while, and, well, you know how it is. I saw her ex sniffing around her and had to lay claim to my girl." Did he sound as much like an idiot as he thought he did?

Adriana pinned him with a shrewd glare. "And how long have you two been seeing each other?"

Damn. Bennett swallowed hard. He made a good chameleon. He'd learned early to be all things to all people. Sweet and sensitive one minute. Aggro hard-ass the next. He was good at reading people and showing them the facets of his personality they needed to see.

What he was not good at, however, was outright lying. It never worked out in his favor, and he preferred not to do it. But he'd started this mess the other night, so there was no backing out now. "It's been on and off for a few months—with our schedules, you know. But we've recently decided to make it exclusive."

She crossed her arms. "Oh, really? How recently? Because I remember Carmela Alvos bragging about how intimate your photo session was."

He held back a groan. Carmela was a bald-faced liar. She'd tried, but he hadn't been interested. Not that he was going to quibble. Because, he had to face it, he had a type. "Nothing happened with Carmela. Val and I just needed some space. Time to work things out."

"Well, that's just…lovely. And you're serious?" Her brow lifted.

Bennett didn't know where this conversation was going, exactly, but it seemed to be headed down Nowhere Good Road and he wasn't having it. "To be honest, I proposed to her last night."

He would have laughed at Adriana's slack-jawed, pinched-nose expression if it didn't mean his future would be in jeopardy.

"Wow. Then I guess congratulations are in order."

"Thank you. She's a great girl." The way he figured it, he'd start traveling soon for Voss and give Adriana a wide berth. She'd never find out the truth.

"That's great. I'd love to get to know her better. Why don't you bring her to the house this weekend for a dinner party we're having?"

Oh, hell. "I'm not sure she's free."

Adriana's eyes narrowed. "Well, *you* can just come."

Not on your life, barracuda. "We'll see what we have going on."

"You do that."

By the time he made his escape, Bennett felt on edge, his skin tight. He needed to get out and shoot. Then he'd feel better. He could take all this shit off-line and breathe for a minute. Thanks to Val, who was a surprisingly good kisser, he'd had a sleepless night on Sunday. And yesterday hadn't been much better. He'd had a catalog shoot in the park, but he hadn't been into it at all. He needed to get his headspace back and away from the two women who were occupying far too much of it.

After a quick subway hop home, he jogged inside just in time to catch the elevator doors as they were closing. "Hey, hold that a second."

The person inside fumbled with something, but Bennett got to the door and held it open just before it closed. Only to find Valentine on the phone and carrying two large grocery bags from the Fresh and Ready on the corner.

She blinked dark eyes up at him, and for a moment, all he could do was stare. How had he never noticed how cute she was before? She was a tiny little thing. Nearly a foot smaller than he was. That put her maybe around five feet three inches, give or take. Her skin was luminescent. Dark and smooth, it reminded him of liquid milk chocolate. Another woman's voice rang in the elevator. "I swear, Valentine, you have to go to these events. You can't just turn up for the wedding. You're needed for the shower, and the rehearsal."

She was talking on speaker, the phone on top of the groceries.

"Mom, I'll call you back, okay?"

"No, not okay. And can you please tell me if James is coming for sure so I can do the place settings? You have been dodging me for months with this. They are going to the engravers tomorrow and I need to know. And while we're at it…"

As the other woman droned on, Valentine's gaze pinned to his and the current of electricity nearly pole-axed him. *Hell.* He needed to get it together. He pushed their floor number again and scooted in next to her.

"Mom, please, let me just—"

"I swear, Valentine, it's like you don't want to spend any time with your family. Let's not forget that you agreed to be part of this wedding, and you living on your own like a recluse in the city, it's just—"

"Mom, please. I *will* call you back."

"You always say that, then I have to chase you down. I mean, that vagabond life you live. Why can't you just use your economics degree and get a job in finance? Or even better, find a man in finance so that you don't have to work. Not like being a blogger is work, mind you."

Bennett shouldn't have been listening. Really. He should have been paying attention to the numbers on the elevator as they went floor by floor. But he was riveted. He watched her face, dying to know how she'd shut down her mother. To be fair, her gaze never left his, either.

"Mom. I love you. I have to go." She tried to use her chin to end the call, but that just sent the bag of groceries tipping over.

With a curse, she tried to recover and the sound of the tearing bag echoed over the walls. Bennett dived for the falling phone and milk. Valentine wobbled in her heels. He saved the milk but not the phone. And not the other bag that followed as Val grabbed for her phone.

Oranges and other fruit rolled onto the floor as a bottle of wine skidded out of her hold.

The good news was, the woman on the phone stopped haranguing her daughter. The bad news was as Val stared at the contents of her bags on the floor, her eyes welled with tears.

Shit. Bennett had a lot of experience with women. A lot. Yes, he was a bit of a man whore. But one thing he was not comfortable with were tears. She just looked so vulnerable, he wanted to tuck her in for a hug. *What the hell is wrong with you?*

When the elevator doors slid open on their floor, he hit the stop button. "Stay here, I'll be right back."

He let himself in to his apartment and grabbed his grocery bags. When he came back in less than a minute, Valentine was desperately trying to gather all her things into her arms.

"Here you go."

She shook her head stiffly. "I think my humiliation

is complete. Thank you. But you don't have to help me. I got this. I can do it."

He merely shrugged. "Everyone needs help sometimes." When he had retrieved the last of the wayward fruit, including some spiked yellow thing he couldn't identify, he stood tall. "Go on, I'm right behind you."

Her phone started to ring on the floor again, and she picked it up but didn't look at it. Just shoved it into her pocket. "Thank you," she muttered. Then she let him into her apartment.

To say he was surprised would have been an understatement. Sure, he'd seen glimpses of her sheer white curtains but he figured given her stiffness, she'd have a sterile beige kind of place. He couldn't be more wrong. Everywhere he turned there was color. Bold and bright. All seamlessly blended together.

"You got it from here?" he asked as she put the bags on the counter.

"Yeah, I'm sorry about the elevator. I'm sort of mortified."

"It happens. Everyone has a bad day from time to time."

"'Kay. Well, see you."

He debated not asking for her help. But as he was here and he needed a hand, too, he might as well. "Okay, so about the other night."

She shook her head. "Oh, we are not doing this conversation. I'm pretending it didn't happen."

"Yeah, well, that's the thing. That woman I was with— that's my boss's wife."

She gasped. "You two were…cozy."

"Yeah, not to my liking. I told her you and I were together to get her off my case, but now she wants to have the two of us for dinner at her place. And given what I heard on the phone, I think maybe the two of us can help each other out."

For one long beat, she stared at him. "You realize this, right here, is the longest conversation we've ever had with each other?"

"What's your point?"

"My point is you don't even know me. But you want me to pretend to be your girlfriend?"

"Fiancée, actually."

A bark of laughter tore out of her. "You're nuts."

"Look, you need a date or whatever to some wedding, it sounds like, and I need a fiancée. This is win-win."

She took the grocery bags and turned them upside down, emptying them before shoving them back at him. "We can't stand each other. You with your tattoos and your loud punk music or whatever."

He frowned. "Excuse me, that's classic rock."

"Whatever. No. You are all wrong. If you have a clean-cut brother, I'm down. But you and I will not mesh. Not to mention that woman looked like she wanted to carve me up into pieces, so thanks, but no thanks."

This was not the end of this conversation. "Okay, well, you think about it."

"Answer's no."

"You want to tell me what you have against me?"

"You mean besides you being arrogant, loud, a womanizer, flirty and accosting me with kisses?"

He smirked. "You liked the kiss, I could tell."

She stormed past him and opened her door. "Out."

With a sigh he turned to go. "I'll give you a couple days to think about it." She rolled her eyes, but as he left, he could have sworn he saw her lips twitch. Well, at least it was a start. He had a few days to wear her down. He wasn't going to the Voss house without her.

* * *

"So tell me exactly what happened. You came home with James, my least favorite friend, and then next thing you know your neighbor's kissing you?"

"I have no idea what happened." Val paced back and forth in her living room in front of the couch as Mel looked up at her. "One second, James was bumbling through a breakup, and the next thing I know Mr. Sexy and Tattooed and Terrible Neighbor was kissing me."

"So exactly *how* did he kiss you?" Mel asked. "Was there tongue, or was it a peck? Did he hold you close up against him? Or was it one of those cases where he just leaned in with his face?"

Val considered. Her mind ran through the kiss over and over again like a movie reel. Bennett with his direct stride and intense focus on her. Bennett wrapping his arm around her waist and sliding one into her hair and then tucking her against him intimately as he lowered his lips. "Yeah, he definitely had me pressed up against him."

Mel hooted. "This is fantastic. Finally, someone we can dig our teeth into who isn't a boring Marcus replacement."

Val frowned at her best friend. They didn't talk about Marcus, since he'd unceremoniously dumped her before her final exams senior year. Val didn't like to reminisce about that period of time. Marcus and everything that came with him was better left forgotten.

Mel held up her hands. "Easy does it. All I'm saying is that ever since Marcus, you've been looking for that perfect Morris Chestnut kind of guy. You know, tall, athletic, charming as hell, great job, the right connections, the right schools. You've pretty much been dating a cookie-cutter version of the same guy for the last five years, and it never works out for you."

"You're wrong. I am not trying to replace Marcus. So what if some of the guys have the same qualities? I happen to *like* those qualities."

Mel shook her head. "No. Your parents like those qualities. You don't know what you like."

"Of course I know what I like." Mel had no idea what she was talking about. Val knew what she liked. Of course she knew what she wanted. She dated. Yes, maybe she aspired for a very specific look. Tall, chocolate and in good shape. That didn't make her super shallow, did it?

"No, you don't. Because you've never dated anything other than the Marcus version. And let me just say, if you're gonna date versions of Marcus, please upgrade. Do not downgrade. That makes no kind of sense. Now, I want to hear more about that sexy neighbor. He sounds like someone completely opposite to Marcus."

Val's stomach flipped at the mere mention of Bennett. Stupid hormones. So what if he made every nerve ending stand up and pay attention? There was more to a relationship than great chemistry. "No, not gonna happen. I don't know what his deal was. But I'm not jumping on the gravy train."

"Of course you're not. Because you never do anything outside of your little box." Before Val could even argue, Mel continued. "You've been saying for the last year how you want to shake up your life. With Sol getting married, you were trying to do your own thing. Break free a little of the usual expectations. What happened in that? Because James was not making that happen. And to make matters worse, *he* was calling *you* boring. How is that even possible?"

Yeah, the jackass had called her boring. That was hardly fair, especially since most times when he talked Val had to fight to stay awake. She hated it that Mel was right. But she had said for her New Year's resolution that she wanted to try something different, something new. For once do things for herself. "Okay, fine. I might have said that, but it's not like I'm not already doing that with my job. I take risks and chances all the time."

"You know that's not what I mean." Mel tucked a lock of hair behind her ear. "You need to supercharge your *life*. Yes, you love your job, but sometimes I feel like one of the reasons you love your job is because you know it makes your family crazy."

"Mel, you know how much I love what I do. I love to eat, and plus, with my nose and my senses, it's a perfect fit." Her nose had always been sensitive, but after an accident at age eight, her sense of smell raced off the charts.

"Fine. I hear you. I just want you to have joy in *all* areas of your life, not just work. And to do that, you're going to have to stop doing the usual and step out of your comfort zone. You are the one who said you wanted to do that. It wasn't me. Let's face it, I'm lazy. I would never have agreed to such a thing for a New Year's resolution. But then again, I don't have sexy tattooed neighbors kissing me."

"Damn, Mel. Do you have to bring him into this every couple of minutes? It's already impossible to think about anything else."

"That's because your subconscious wants to think about him. Honey, would it hurt to do something different? What would you have to lose? Worst case scenario, you march over there asking why he kissed you, he says he doesn't know, he was bored, then you two make out like a couple of teenagers."

Val had to laugh at that. Mel could be ridiculous. But she also had a point. She wanted to shake up her life—

well, this was one way to do it. "Fine, I'll talk to neighbor boy. Are you happy now?"

"I won't be happy unless you take him to Sol's wedding and tell me he has a twin."

Chapter 4

Nobody in their right mind would believe that Val was dating someone like Bennett. Nobody. Especially not her parents.

As she posted her latest review of a restaurant on Spring Street that did a killer Thai avocado salad, she glared at the wedding invitation pinned to her calendar.

Yes, she needed a date, but that guy? He had helped her with her groceries, and he was right, James was a jerk. And the look of irritation and annoyance on James's face had been well worth it. But the most irritating part was that he was an excellent kisser. And he knew it.

That's because the man has kissed a lot of women. She'd seen him. It wasn't even speculation. More times than she could count, she'd seen him practically mauling some leggy model in his doorway.

Not that she could blame them. The man radiated sex appeal. But in no way was he appropriate. Like, at all.

And she was way past the irritate-Daddy-with-my-new-boyfriend phase of her life. Not that she'd ever had that. She'd been the good one. Not that that ever made her parents happy. She'd bring home an A, her mother would ask why wasn't it an A-plus. She'd make the lacrosse team, she'd ask why she wasn't team captain. Never mind how great she was. She wasn't good enough. Her father, while stern was warmer. Sometimes, he'd find her after her mother had just put her through the ringer and ask if she'd done her best. When she said yes, he'd say, "Great, then I'm proud of you."

And truth was, she'd made things easy on her parents. She didn't buck the system. She never met a rule or regulation that she didn't follow.

Until, of course, instead of using her economics degree she'd started her own business. Blogging about food, no less. Her lifestyle brand had really started to take off during her last year at NYU. It was one thing to post funny commentary on ingredients. It was another thing to have people pay her for those opinions.

Val shut down her laptop and climbed into bed, carefully wrapping her hair in a satin scarf. After her career choice, she was pretty sure her mother would have an aneurysm if she showed up with someone like Bennett. What did he do, anyway? An artist or photographer, she wasn't really sure. Hell, he could have been a badass biker who ran a motorcycle club, and she'd have no clue. *Really time to get to know your neighbors better.*

She didn't mean to be a recluse. Well, not really. And maybe she *was* a bit rigid. But it was often easier to stay in her routine than change it. She'd taken enough risk in her life, thank you very much.

Val turned over and punched her pillow, picturing Bennett's tempting smirk. Why was the man so infuriating? Something low in her belly pulled, and she groaned against the need.

No, she would not do this. Especially not because his raw sex appeal woke up everything inside her that screamed, *Hello, I'm a woman*. Again she repeated all the reasons why his little proposal was a bad idea. Artist. Unconventional. *White*. They wouldn't have a fundamental problem with him being white, but the fact that he was different from every single man they'd shoved at her would rankle her mother. And well, he screamed bad boy.

No way her parents were going to let him in the door. They were professors at Princeton, for the love of God. Their tenured friends would wrinkle their little upturned noses when they saw him. And that would earn another disapproving glare from her mother. Oh, how Val had become accustomed to that glare.

Outside all that, she had her own reasons. She didn't like him, for one. For two, he was obnoxious. And arrogant. Nobody would believe she would even look at him. Much less be *engaged* to him.

But he kissed better than any man had the right to, and she'd promised herself she'd do something different. Try something different. And if this wasn't a shining beacon as to why she needed to, she didn't know what was. Who gave a flying fig what anyone thought? She wasn't going home alone. Just once she wanted to tell everyone to shut up. She didn't care. Bringing Bennett home would certainly do that.

Val sat up and pulled the scarf off her head. She didn't even pause as she opened her door and charged right up to his. If she hesitated, she'd think this through. She'd worry too much. She'd think about all the bad things, all the angles. She knocked briskly three times.

Though, given the soul-shaking decibels of Joe

Cocker, she doubted he heard her. When he didn't come, she knocked again. It took him another minute before he yanked open the door…shirtless. Wearing only a pair of jeans hanging very low on his waist.

Val could only stare. Damn. She'd only ever seen anybody this good-looking naked in a magazine. She was a food blogger, and sure, she worked with models. But they didn't need to be shirtless to pose with food. *Note to self, start requiring shirtless male models.* His tattoos, roped and corded around his arms and his torso, were a beautiful thing to see. She wanted to run her fingertips over them.

"Hey, sweetheart, my eyes, they're up here."

She snapped her gaze to his and flushed, hoping her dark complexion would conceal her embarrassment. "Okay, fine. I'll scratch your back if you'll scratch mine. But a couple of things first."

"Of course there's a catch," he whispered. His lips tipped into a lopsided smile, and she almost forgot what the hell she was saying. She should make a no-smiling rule.

Because that smile would get her in trouble. "First, turn your music down. We might be the only ones on this floor, but seriously, I need my beauty rest. Second, we need some rules of engagement. Finally, don't call me *sweetheart.*"

He leaned forward, and she involuntarily swayed toward him, his scent intoxicating her. "Whatever you say, cookie."

Chapter 5

Bennett studied Valentine as they sat in the café connected to their building. "You know, you can loosen up a little, right? I don't bite or anything." He smirked. "Unless you're into that sort of thing. In which case I might reconsider." He gave her what he hoped was a disarming smile. But nothing. All she gave him were dark eyes widened to the size of saucers. "Come on, Valentine. Give me something to work with here."

When she wrinkled her nose, he had to smile. She probably didn't realize the action made her look adorable. He wasn't going to be the one to tell her, though.

"Sorry. This is somehow more awkward than every first date I've ever been on. And for me that's saying something."

"Look, I go on a lot of first dates."

"Somehow that does not surprise me," she muttered under her breath.

He opened his mouth in mock shock. "Oh, my God, was that an attempt at snark or humor? Be still my heart. I might be in love."

That did it—a giggle escaped, transforming her normally stoic face into one that completely arrested him. Wow. Her full smile could easily be a weapon of mass destruction for men everywhere. He should call somebody about that or something. Report it. What was that campaign the MTA was putting out there? If you see something, say something? Valentine Anderson was lethal. Thing was, he was pretty sure she didn't know it.

"Okay, well, you can call me Val. I hate the name Valentine. And these days it's more of a curse thing anyway."

"That's too bad. I think it's cute, but Val it is. So, Val, what do you say we actually go somewhere, do something? We can head uptown to the Met or to Central Park. Or we can stay down here and check out the Moore Gallery. It just opened and—"

She stammered as she interrupted him. "Y-you want to go to the Moore Gallery?"

He frowned at that. "Yeah. I love art. I *am* a photographer. I like to look at beautiful things."

She put up a hand. "Sorry. I guess until yesterday, I wasn't even really sure you were a photographer. I assumed artist, but even then, like a welding artist or glassblower or something. I kept trying to pair the loud music with you."

"Glassblower, huh?" He laughed. "I kinda like that idea. I should totally photograph that. Sorry to disappoint, though."

"It's okay." She shrugged. "At one point I also convinced myself that you were the leader of a motorcycle gang and you were running a black market operation or something out of your loft."

"I like how you think." He nodded toward her untouched coffee. "You want to get that in a to-go cup so we can leave and check out the gallery? Beats sitting here trying to get all our details written down. We can make it more organic."

She raised a brow. "Like a *real* first date?"

The hairs on the back of his neck stood up in warning. Was she indicating that she wanted this to be a real date? This was not part of the dozen or so scenarios he'd run. "Uh, not really."

She barked out a laugh, and damn it, his brain did that misfire, unfocused thing again. "Oh, my goodness, you should see your face right now. Relax, slick. I don't want to date you any more than you want to date me. You are not my type in any way, shape or comprehensible form."

He frowned. *Wait, why are you upset? You don't want to be her type.* Yeah, but still. He was every woman's type. Evidence being how he ended up here in the first place. "Uh, that's a first, but whatever."

"We can leave the coffee. I can't drink it anyway." She stood.

"Why not? Something wrong with it?" He followed.

She shook her head. "I'll have that bitter taste on my tongue all damn afternoon and I won't be able to eat, because I can taste the burned citrus flavor of the beans. It'll make me nuts."

"Seriously? You don't like coffee?"

"Oh, I love coffee, I just need it to be good coffee. Otherwise I can't taste anything else. And for a food blogger, that's disastrous."

He frowned. "First of all, what do you mean, good coffee? Second of all, how is it that I didn't know you're a food blogger?"

She shrugged. "You pay much attention to lifestyle brands?"

"I'm a photographer, remember?"

"Yeah, good point."

He opened the door for her and had to grit his teeth when she brushed by him lightly. *Hell.* This hormonal thing was going to be a problem. *Relax, it'll go away.* Soon enough, he'd be on assignment…he hoped, anyway. On assignment he could sleep with a whole bunch of women to block out the taste of her. Right now, though, damn. "What's your handle or whatever?"

"I'm Val's Heart."

He stopped in his tracks. "Seriously? You've been in a few national magazines. You had an article on ethnic food we've been missing or something like that."

She grinned. "You saw that?"

"Well, I was helping out the art director for layout with some of the spare photos I'd done. I went to that Eritrean restaurant you recommended in Brooklyn."

The wonder in her eyes and her smile were completely infectious. "Wow. Someone who knows me. That's great."

"Well, lots of people know you. You're in magazines."

"Yeah, I guess, logically I know that, but it's not like I meet someone and I'm all, *I'm Val's Heart,* you know."

"I guess so. So tell me, where is this great coffee? And why won't you be able to eat anything else?"

She grinned as she led the way down Prince Street. "I sort of have a combination of hyperosmia and synesthesia. The hyperosmia I was born with, though it intensified when the synesthesia started. It's like I can taste and smell everything. Everything has a scent. Coffee, for example, is extremely strong. If it's not the good stuff, I'll be tasting the bitter aftertaste for the rest of the day. And

I'll be able to smell it nonstop. Not to mention I wouldn't be able to do anything else with my taste buds."

"That's amazing. So everything has a specific odor?"

She nodded. "Sometimes it can be great. Like when you walk into one of those high-end chocolatiers where they do shavings for you? Man, that place is like pure nosegasm."

A laugh burst forth. "Did you just say nosegasm?"

She nodded. "Sure did. It's a thing. At least to me it's a thing. It's easy to get overwhelmed, too. If I'm not mentally prepared, or I don't have my nose plugs, large crowds will give me a headache like no other. Also, a night out at a cramped club or something with my girl-friends can be hazardous. Bigger venues can be better as long as they're nice and airy. But a lot of guys put on way too much cologne."

He knew he shouldn't ask the question, but his curiosity got the better of him. "What do I smell like?"

Her answer was immediate. "Sandalwood and musk, and there's something like the hint of the ocean. It's a fresher scent. I can't really place it."

"So is that good or bad?" Why did his voice sound so husky?

"It's, uh—" A faint hint of pink tinged her cheeks, and he had to smile. So he smelled good to her, huh? Why the hell was that a good thing? "You know. For people who like sandalwood, it's great. Come on, let me show you what real coffee tastes like."

His next question died on his tongue. *Do* you *like sandalwood?*

So Bennett Cooper wasn't *all* bad. And if Val was being honest with herself, she'd had fun. A really good time. The gallery was just the icebreaker she'd needed.

It was easier to be free with him when they were walking and talking.

And while he might not be the best neighbor, he was smart. Quite brilliant. The man had been all over the world. He was talking about an expedition to the North Pole next. Once they'd started on travel and food, they pretty much hadn't stopped talking.

So maybe trying something new hadn't been the end of the world. Val still wasn't convinced taking him home was the best idea she'd ever had. And he still was not her type, but he was almost cool. *Almost.* And it wouldn't be awkward.

When the elevator let them out on their floor, he hesitated, then mumbled, "Oh, great. Our first test."

"Isn't that your lady friend from the other night?"

He gave her a pursed-lip smirk. "She's not my lady friend. Try my boss's wife."

"She seriously putting the moves on you?"

"You could say that."

"Who's the guy with her?" The man casually leaning against Bennett's door was more like the kind of guy Val should take home. Dark chocolate skin, pretty as hell, and dressed to kill in a blazer and dark jeans. She knew fashion well enough to recognize that the jacket was Marc Jacobs. The shoes were Louboutins for men. The dude practically screamed *I'm a model.*

"That is my best friend, Trevor. He's back from a stint in Europe. Making New York his home base again."

"Right. Okay." She plastered a smile on her face. "So how do you want to do this?"

He ran his hand through his hair. "Follow my lead."

"Wait, wha—"

But his fingers clasped around hers and he tugged her down the hall before she could argue.

"Trev, my man. Welcome home." He released Val only long enough to wrap his arms around the other man and clap him hard on the back. "When did you get back?"

Trevor grinned at Bennett just before his gaze flickered over Val. "This morning. But I'm guessing I should have called first. Who's your friend?"

She stiffened. And this was where she'd have to pull this off. With a deep breath, she slipped into character. "I'm Val, Bennett's fiancée. You must be Trevor. I've heard a lot about you." She turned her attention to Adriana. "And you're Mrs. Voss, right? I'm sorry we didn't get to meet properly the other night. You know Bennett—sometimes he gets carried away."

Adriana's face pinched, making her look like a duck who'd sucked on a lemon. Trevor, on the other hand, grinned even as he stared at Bennett. "Yo, man, we have a lot to catch up on. I move to Europe for six months and you go and fall in love?" He added, "And you, Val, we're going to talk, because if you can rope my man Bennett here, you are formidable and I want to marry your sister." His gaze slid over her. "Tell me you have a sister."

Bennett just shook his head. "Dude, shut up. Adriana, did we have an appointment? I'd hate to think I missed something."

The older woman looked none too pleased. "I'm actually just here to extent the invitation to dinner this weekend to Val myself. I figured you might forget or not tell her how genuinely we want to meet this fiancée of yours."

Wow. She was a piece of work. Translation: she didn't believe the ruse. Fair enough. If Val was going to be Bennett's fiancée, she might as well go all in. "Oh, he told me, Mrs. Voss. And I'm delighted to say we'll be able to make it. Unfortunately, though, I have a long day tomorrow, so I can't stay and chat. Baby, I'll see you tomorrow?" She slid her hand over Bennett's abs to his pecs, and his eyes darkened.

"You guys avert your gaze. I'm going to kiss my fiancée good-night now." He walked her to the door, and Val only had seconds to brace herself. She opened her door and tried to center her mind. *This is not real. This is not real. This. Is. Not. Real.*

But when Bennett dragged her to him and dipped his head, her lady parts forgot all about the mantra. Her libido screamed, *Hell, yes, this feels real.* His hand slid into her hair and he tugged gently as he anchored her head.

When his tongue delved in, the sweetness hit her first. And she wanted to indulge. Wanted to take her time and savor. He ratcheted up the heat by flexing the hand at her waist, and she gasped softly.

It was Trevor's low whistle that broke the spell. When Bennett drew back, he looked like he was having a hard time keeping his eyes open. "I'll see you later," she croaked.

"Oh, you can count on that. Good night, Valentine. Sweet dreams."

"Dude, you want to tell me what the hell that was all about?"

Bennett ran his hands through his hair as he tossed his bag on his living room couch. "Don't even get me started."

Trevor knew exactly where the imported beer was kept and helped himself. "No, no, I need to know. Inquiring minds and all that. Last I left you, two months ago, you were with that blonde in Sweden, but you were a confirmed bachelor. You were never, *ever* going for a girlfriend or wife. Now I come home and you not only have a fiancée—with no ring, might I add—but you also have some hot MILF looking like she wants to kill your fine-as-hell fiancée."

Trevor shifted around Bennett, plopped himself onto his couch and kicked his feet up onto the low stainless steel coffee table. "Bennett, you have some 'splaining to do. And just FYI, not white 'splaining, either. You gotta get me to the nitty-gritty here."

Bennett couldn't help a chuckle. Shit, he'd missed Trevor. He sank down on the couch and grabbed the beer his friend held out. "The MILF, as you called her, that's my new boss's wife, Adriana Voss. She somehow has it in her head that this is the ride she wants to get on at the fair." He gestured at his body.

Trevor nodded sagely. "That is a reputation well cultivated over the last decade or more. All women want to experience the Bennett Cooper ride."

All except his neighbor. "Yeah, well, Voss Magazines is exactly where I want to be. So many options as a photographer. The magazine I want to do the most is obviously—"

"Earth," his best friend finished for him. When Bennett cocked his head, Trevor merely shrugged. "We've been friends since you moved upstate with your aunt. You think I don't know you want to be a wildlife photographer like your dad?"

That piece of knowledge both warmed Bennett and made him uncomfortable. He cultivated this facade—charming, funny, but not too deep or close—for years. It always unsettled him when people saw past that. Even if that person was Trevor.

"Yeah, I guess you would know that. Anyway. Adriana's been getting a little too drunk at parties. Way too close. Things she says are starting to border on inappropriate. I'm no dummy, so I've been keeping a wide berth. I like my job. I've worked hard for my job. Anyway, Adriana crashes a meeting I had downstairs at True North and she wants to see the self nudes I did last year."

Trevor hooted and cackled. "Bennett Cooper, you are a bad boy."

"Dude." Bennett shook his head. "There was no way around it. That woman is persistent as hell."

Trevor leaned forward. "Yo." He pinned him with a direct glare. "You tap that?"

Trevor and he had the same no-cheaters rule. Trevor had honed his after years of watching his poor mother get cheated on again and again by Trevor's father, a former NFL player. "No, man, what do I look like to you? I'm a single man but I have standards."

Trevor nodded. "How'd you escape with your virtue, then?"

Bennett took a long pull of his beer. "Uh, see, what had happened was…" He let his voice trail off as Trevor laughed. "Okay, so I had to think quick. She was coming up the elevator, wrapping herself around me boa constrictor–style, and Val was getting the brush-off from some dude, so I killed two birds with one stone. Walked right up to her and kissed her, pretending we were together."

Trevor stared at him. Once again he was reminded of why his friend was so popular with photographers and designers. There was an intensity to him. But there was also a glimmer of mischief and humor just under the surface. Trevor fell back laughing so hard he clutched his sides.

"Yeah, yeah, laugh it up. I need your advice, and you're mocking me."

"Nah, man. For real, though. Only *you* would get yourself into this mess. I have always told you the D would get you in a heap of trouble."

"This from the guy who slept his way through half the models in Barcelona."

Trevor grinned. "What can I say? I'm pretty."

"Pretty bastard." Bennett laughed. "So, what do I do?"

His friend shrugged. "You and neighbor lady seem on good terms, and she saved your ass with that dinner invite."

"Well, up until that day, we'd barely spoken. Turns out she needs a date to some wedding or whatever in a few weeks."

"So quid pro quo then."

Bennett nodded. "Yep. And maybe I'll be out of here on assignment after I complete my end of the bargain, so no chance of her getting too attached."

Trevor slid him a glance. "So the sparks I saw out there, that was nothing?"

"What? No. I barely know the woman."

"She is choice, though. Looks like petite brown Barbie. I mean, did you see the rack on her? She could…"

Bennett loved Trevor. He was the brother he had always wanted. But the surge of jealousy had his jaw clenching and him shaking his head. "Don't, Trev."

His best friend's forehead wrinkled. "Well, well, maybe that thing with your neighbor isn't just a mutual favor after all?"

Bennett scrubbed a hand down his face. What was wrong with him? "No. I mean, yes." *Hell.* "Look, she's not all that bad. But she's a nice person, so let's cool it on the ogling her assets."

"Fair enough." Trevor nodded. "Backing off, but can I ask you a question, man?"

"Shoot."

"What if it wasn't just a quid-pro-quo thing? With

her? What if…it could be something real? You give that any thought?"

"Of course not. I'm not looking for anything. You know that. I'm a free agent. I can't be tied down." He'd had maybe one three-month relationship in college. And another six-month stint right out of school, but neither one had stuck. His travel made it impossible. And to be honest, they were barely relationships. More like sex on tap with the occasional dinner or drinks thrown in. He'd never introduced a woman to Trevor or his aunt. He'd always known they wouldn't be staying.

Trevor nodded. "I hear you. But maybe you like this one. I've been present for you kissing a lot of girls. Remember Mindy Tabsy in the seventh grade? I've never seen you be even remotely possessive about anyone. I'll let it go, but I'm just saying. You seem different."

"I promise you, Trev, I'm exactly the same." Bennett was not a permanent kind of guy. And certainly not with someone as uptight as Val. Even if today there'd been nothing uptight about her.

Chapter 6

Focus was the name of the game. All Val had to do was concentrate, right? Except she could barely function. She'd slept like crap because she was thinking about Bennett. And his lips. And how insane he looked with his shirt off. Damn it. She dragged her attention back to her meeting with Mr. Rollins.

"Valentine, I'm sure you'll see the contract with Emmerson Branding is a great deal. You'll discuss their products, back them up. Your followers trust what you have to say," said Mr. Rollins.

She looked over the contract again. It sure had a lot of zeros. But she wasn't going into this blind. She knew how this worked. Emmerson Branding wanted a yes-person who was going to promote all of their products. She'd be nothing more than a spokesperson for every product they had. She'd built a reputation as a smart and savvy blogger with lots of followers. Every now and again companies wanted to pay her to promote their products. Lately she'd gotten more restrictive about what she would endorse.

While she primarily focused on food, she did still do lifestyle blogging.

"I'm sorry but these stipulations are too restrictive for me, and we've discussed this before. People appreciate that I'm telling them the truth. And with this deal, it requires I say nothing negative, so that's just not going to work out. Because if the product tastes like an ammonia and vinegar cocktail, I'm going to say so. And they stipulate *right* here that I can't say that. I can say nothing. But I can't not speak the truth. Moreover, what's really worrisome is that the wording is such that seems like they might compel me to say something. Something I don't believe."

When she'd started on Vid Tube in college, she'd mostly reviewed restaurants. Then hair products, makeup. All kinds of things that she used on a daily basis. Her passion, though, was food. She spent more time doing that than anything else. Before she knew it, her blog received so much traffic she was able to charge advertising fees.

Once out of school, she'd transitioned to lifestyle blogging, too. The women's magazines came next and all she had to do was write about her experience. As gigs went, it was like a dream come true. Finally something she could use her uniqueness for, which didn't include being locked in a lab all day. Most people like her, she heard about, worked in perfumeries.

"Mr. Rollins, unless you can remove these troublesome clauses, I don't think we can work together. Which would be a shame, because I like a lot of what Emmerson is doing. But some products, on the other hand, simply don't work, and I need the freedom to be able to say so."

She gathered her purse, phone and tablet. He rose. "I

appreciate you considering working with us. I'll take it back to them."

"Look, I'm not trying to be difficult. But it's about my brand. If I'm pairing myself with a company, it has to be the right deal. Like a marriage."

No. The last thing she needed to think about was weddings or wedding dates. Because that brought her right back to Bennett. Her body flushed and she forced a smile. "Give me a call when they're ready."

As she walked out of the office, the massive wall photo in the lobby caught her attention. There was something so familiar about what appeared to be a woman dancing in the center of the sun. Before she left she asked the receptionist, "Excuse me, do you know who took that photo?"

The receptionist smiled. "Oh, yeah, that's from that hot photographer. He was in *People*'s sexiest issue. Not the cover or anything, but he got a mention. He took it. What was his name? Benji. Benny… Oh, yeah. Bennett Cooper."

"Bennett Cooper?" Val's eyes went wide.

"Yeah, that's the one. Mr. Emmerson got it at auction. He was so excited. It went for nearly half a million or something."

Val stared at the image. The guy she'd thought ran a motorcycle club was world-class. Just who was she pretending to date, anyway?

Val found her mother waiting at their usual table at Akasha. Her mother was nothing if not a creature of habit. They'd been having lunch at Akasha once a month since Val left for NYU. They'd always sat at the same table, and for the most part ordered the same things. Her mother would go on about how great her sister was, all the while telling Val how she'd just missed out on being great. Ah, the joys of routine.

"Hi, Mom."

Her mother's smile was brief. "Honey, are you still parting your hair to the side like that? I told you you have to vary your parts or it causes stress on the hairline." She sighed. "Not that you'll ever listen. Anyway. You're late."

"Actually, I'm five minutes early." Val didn't even glance at her watch, but she was never late for a lunch with her mother. She'd never hear the end of it. These lunches had become such a routine that Val knew exactly how to start the conversation to get her mother talking so she could mentally plan the rest of her day. "How are the wedding plans?"

And they were off. With an exaggerated roll of her eyes, her mother started in on the caterers and the alcohol and how it really was tacky to do a cash bar, but it was also alarming to have people sloshing around drunk at their perfect baby's wedding. And then it went to the dress and the fittings and why Val had been MIA during the fitting.

Val didn't bother to remind her mother that she wasn't the maid of honor or even a bridesmaid. Not that she and her sister were feuding.

They just weren't close, and had a distant relationship. Sol was seven years younger, so Val had been more mother figure than sister. And her sister had her friends and her own instincts. Besides, they were different. Where Val toed the line, followed the rules, Sol did not. She sneaked out, made out with boys, took their father's car on a joyride. Went to concerts. And did the things that said, *Hey, I've lived life.* Val hadn't really done any of that. She hadn't spread her wings at all until she was in college and on her own. And even then she was restrained. She really did need to get a life.

When her mother veered to the topic of her date, Val desperately tried to recover the threads of the conversation so she could piece together what she'd missed. "Actually, Mom, I've been meaning to tell you, James and I broke up."

Dear old Mom didn't miss a beat, sighing and throwing her napkin down. "Honestly, Val, it's like you're trying to drive these men away from you with a flame-thrower. Why did this one break up with you? It's like we can't get you a foothold with the man thing. It's probably because you're too aloof. Men like warmth in a woman. It's not your nose thing, is it? I thought it was mostly under control."

Val ground her teeth. "No. It wasn't my *nose thing.*" From the moment she'd been hit, things had gotten increasingly difficult with her parents. So many places she couldn't go. All the weird things she said about how food tasted funny. She really hadn't helped her parents make any new friends. "And *I* broke up with him." *There.* That was sort of the truth.

The look on her mother's face was priceless. "But why in heavens would you do that? He is *the* James Adamson. He is old New Orleans—his great-great-grandfather was a freedman who became a doctor. In those times. Can you imagine his pedigree? He's an *Adamson.* A young black man who's carrying on the family tradition. He's a dermatologist. Renowned. His earning potential is huge. Honestly, I don't understand you sometimes."

As her mother spoke, all the reasons why Val wanted a change in the first place bubbled to the surface. She wanted freedom of choice. She wanted to do something because she craved it and not because it was expected. She wanted to want someone because it lit her on fire.

Like Bennett. No. Not like Bennett. But whatever. She just didn't want bland. Not anymore. She was in charge of her life and she could do what she liked. "Actually, Mom, I do have somebody. It's new, but it's serious."

Her mother arched delicate brows. "Oh? Do tell. Who is his family? Where did they go to university? Do I know them? Did he do Jack and Jill?"

Shoot, that was information she didn't have. Why hadn't she prepped better? *Because you were too busy reveling in the way Bennett tastes and not paying attention to the information you need to deliver.* "Mom, you don't know him. You might know his work, though. He's a photographer." Cue the nose wrinkle. Ooh, was that just her, or was there a snort, too? Awesome.

"A photographer? Sweetheart. You don't seem to understand. Who you date, and eventually who you marry, matters. You're a descendant of Garrett Morgan, an inventor and successful businessman. Think about that. You want to be with someone who is *just* a photographer?"

"Mom, why is it the first question you ask is about his lineage and not if I'm happy? Which I am, by the way."

Her mother waved her hands to dismiss her. "This is still salvageable. If we just do some research, maybe his family is somebody and…"

Val only just managed to hide the shudder snaking up her spine. "No. Mom. No background checks. No checks to see if he's got any Links members in his family. No check of the Jack and Jill database. None of that. He's a photographer and pretty well-known. And he's my neighbor. We've been dating a few months, but it's getting pretty serious, so he'll be coming to the wedding with me." She held her breath. The Links and Jack and Jill were the black community status markers her mother used to see if dating prospects were to be taken seriously.

Her mother's lips formed a small O, and Val wanted to laugh. Well, that certainly did the trick. She'd never said no to her mother before. Not in any meaningful way. Well, that wasn't true. She'd picked her own career—though to be fair, the parental units still thought she was going to quit and pursue finance.

"Well, you certainly don't have to raise your voice at me. I'm just looking out for you. Making sure you get the bes—"

"Valentine?" They both turned to see who had interrupted her mother, and Val's heart sank. *James.* What the hell was he doing here? He was going to ruin everything. "James?"

He studied her closely. "I thought that was you. I had a meeting with a medical rep."

She prayed he didn't want to talk, but from the looks of it, that's exactly what he wanted. "You remember my mother?"

"Yes, of course. Mrs. Anderson, how are you?"

"Well, I was fine until I heard that the two of you parted ways. I'm terribly sorry. You know how Valentine can be. I certainly have high hopes that you two can patch things up."

"Actually that's why I came over, Valentine."

"I told you, *Val.*" Her parents were one thing—they'd picked her ridiculous name. And somehow when Bennett said it, it didn't sound contrived. But James needed to learn to call her Val.

"Fine, *Val*, I don't like how we left things the other night. I'd like to speak to you. Maybe when you're done with your mother."

Her mother pushed her chair back. "Nonsense, dear, you two kids talk. I'll make a call."

"Mom, sit. James, we have nothing to say to each other." Had he forgotten that he'd been the one fumbling through dumping her?

"Val, listen, I know that maybe we both lost a little focus, but if we—"

Focus? Was that what he called trying to break up with her? Losing focus? But now that she had Bennett, he wanted her. *Correction, you do not have Bennett.* Have, fake have, same difference. "No." Wow, she was starting to like the word. "I'm with Bennett now. I've made that clear."

"But with our families and our shared backgrounds, I make a better fit for you than some white boy with tattoos."

And just like that the cat was out of the bag.

Chapter 7

Why was he nervous?

Bennett was never nervous. Hell, he spent most of his life doing crazy things like jumping out of a plane to get the right picture or talking himself into some forbidden place to get the perfect shot. But now, he was anxious.

All because Val was poking around his pics. She stopped at the one on his back wall and pointed to it. "This one. I saw it in the lobby of an office building yesterday. I knew I'd seen it before. I guess I didn't realize I'd seen it here. When you open your door it's visible from the hall." She turned back to "Dancing in the Sun."

"It's one of my favorites. I took that one in Bali. There was a woman—a girl, really. She was young. She'd been standing in direct sunlight dancing in the middle of this temple. It was so beautiful I had to shoot it. I knew I would never get another shot like it."

"You've been all over the world."

"Oh, come on. You think I didn't look you up? You've been all over the world, too," Bennett said as he leaned against his island.

"Yes. But something tells me your trips were a little less sanitized than mine." He barked a laugh, and she flushed. "No, that's not what I meant. I just meant you're an off-the-beaten-path kind of guy. I'm a five-star-hotels kind of girl."

Bennett shook his head. "No, that fits. There are a lot of places that I didn't want to lay my head down, but I still went, chasing that incredible shot. The magnificent sunrise."

She narrowed her gaze. "Oh, so you're chasing the green flash or something?"

She was witty. Smart. Inquisitive. It made him edgy. "Not exactly. But something like that. Ever since I could pick up a camera, I knew this was what I wanted to do."

"Your work. It's beautiful, Bennett. Really."

A flush crept up his neck. "Thank you. This is everything I am."

Val moved from piece to piece, studying. "So you know James?"

He frowned. "James?"

She sighed. "My ex with the sweater-vest?"

"Ah, yes. That jerk."

"Yeah, well, when I was having lunch with my mom he showed up and broke our news."

He shrugged. "Well, isn't that the point?"

"Yes, but, I wanted you to slide in under the radar. But James leaked the information to Mom and she pretty much flipped out, so she'll be coming at you hard. We need to tighten this up. She asked me a bunch of questions about you. Questions I couldn't answer. I mean, I know your name. I know you're a photographer. But hell, I didn't even know you were a big deal."

"Does it matter?" Again, the hairs on the back of his neck stood up. This was what worried him. If she found out the truth, would that change how she looked at him? It shouldn't matter. But for a reason he didn't want to examine, he didn't want her to find out who his parents were. He didn't want that kind of complication. He swallowed hard as he watched her closely.

"No, it doesn't matter to me. Hell, a week ago, I hated you."

"Ouch. *Hate* is a very strong word, Valentine."

"Yes, it's a strong word. But you have to admit you were the worst neighbor." She laughed.

He shrugged. "Maybe."

She stood in front of him, all five feet three inches of her, and ticked off the reasons on her fingers. "Maybe?"

"Oh, come on who doesn't like the Rolling Stones and Aerosmith?"

"They're fine, but at those decibels? Come on."

He shrugged. "Fine. What do you need to know?"

"Tell me something about your family. My mother will ask."

He shifted uncomfortably. "What about them?"

"Parents. I assume you have them."

What to tell her… "They died when I was a kid. My aunt raised me." That was the truth.

"I'm sorry." She looked down at her hands. "I didn't know."

"How could you?" In an attempt to deflect the too-personal question, he asked, "What about you?"

"Professors. Both of them."

"Wow, okay. Must make you a brainiac. They're probably really proud of you."

She stopped in front of a photo of the night sky he'd captured in Alaska during the aurora. "No, actually. Once I had the accident, they weren't too thrilled to have me around. I made things...difficult for them."

Bennett frowned as he leaned against the wall. "What accident?"

She tapped her nose. "This didn't happen until I was eight or so. There was an accident with a baseball. Had to have surgery. After, I was too aware of every smell. I was a mild synesthete before, but after, it's like the sensations exploded all around me." She shrugged. "It made things really hard for them."

"That's bullshit, they're your parents. And that is amazing. But I don't know much about it."

"It's rare, but my version of synesthesia is a heightened awareness of tastes and smells. So if I smell chocolate, I taste it as well. Anyway, my sister, Solstice. She was sick a lot as a baby. My parents doted on her and hovered over her as a baby. I thought if I could be perfect it would make up somehow for all those hospital trips. But instead, I was the family freak."

Bennett shook his head. "You are not a freak, and you're not responsible for your condition. And you're not responsible for your sister."

"Come on, Bennett. You want to tell me your parents being gone doesn't motivate you to be the best that you can? You're saying it doesn't drive you?"

That hit far too close to home for his liking, and he took a deep breath. "How is she now? Your sister."

Her smile was slight. "Great. It's her wedding, actually. She got to have the kind of adolescence I wished I'd had. You know free, rebellious."

"The adolescence you wished you'd had?"

She wrinkled her nose. "That sounds bad when I say

it out loud, doesn't it? I feel selfish for wishing that. Because she had it rough as a baby, my parents just let her do whatever she wanted. I'm not the rebellious type. Obviously. But I promised myself I was going to do new things. Try different activities." She shrugged. "Hanging out with you seems to accomplish my goal."

"So, you're all in then?"

"I am." She nodded. "I don't think I knew that until I saw my mother's face. She'd rather I do the puppet thing. Say the right things, do the right things. Be with the *right* people." She used air quotes for "right."

"What do *you* want?"

"To be honest, I haven't the foggiest. But I don't want to do this anymore." She threw up her hands. "I want to be different. And not just in word, but in what I do and the steps I take. I'm never going to get everything I want out of life if I don't embrace it fully."

Bennett grinned. "Well, you've come to the right place. Adventure and new experiences are my middle names."

Chapter 8

"So you're telling me I don't get to meet her properly."

Bennett angled the camera to capture Trevor. "Hold still, I'm trying to get the shot." Click. "And you've already met her." Click. He climbed down the ladder, and Trevor turned to look at him. The latest Brazilian it girl shifted down Trevor's body and gave him an impish smile. Click.

His best friend didn't even miss a beat. Trevor gave her a look that was somewhere between smoldering and mischievous. Click.

"Come on. I want to see what she's all about."

"And I said, what's the point? You know the situation." He kept things vague, because he didn't know if Adriana Voss had spies anywhere. And for the next couple of weeks he was in full fiancée mode.

"I just want to meet the girl my boy is about to say *I do* to." Trevor grinned, looking every bit the *GQ* cover model he was. Click.

Bennett stood to his full height and called for a set change. Trevor helped the girl up, and he and Bennett escaped to the balcony so Trevor could smoke. "Okay, man, I don't understand why not. Bring me in on the charade. It looks weird if your best friend is not friends with your fiancée."

"Why does it matter? You want to hit on her?"

"She's mad cute. If you're serious and it's just a quid-pro-quo thing, then what's the problem?"

Bennett locked his jaw. "No problem. She's just busy and prickly. I'm not sure you two would mesh."

"Uh-huh. Or is it that the great Bennett Cooper has a thing for his neighbor with the juicy booty?"

He glared at Trevor. If the guy wasn't his friend, he'd find him extremely annoying. "I don't. But you can't hit on her, either."

His friend laughed. "Relax, man. You should see your face when I talk about getting close to her. We've never been in a fight, but I can tell that while I have my excellent musculature on my side, you have sheer possessive anger going for you. You want that girl."

He was not being possessive. Trevor was just a player. Val was not looking for that. *How would you know what she's looking for?* Trevor was the kind of guy who fit with what she'd said her parents wanted. "It's not like that."

"Right. So why haven't you taken a single number today? The model from this morning—man, that woman practically threw her boobs in your face. And Lena, that Brazilian girl, was supposed to flirt with me, but instead, every look was for the camera. Or you." He winked.

"Well, maybe she was doing her job. She's supposed to make love to the camera."

"Whatever, man. I think you have a thing for little

Miss Uptight and Proper. And I want to examine her. See if she's gonna be good for you."

"Whatever. You want to spill all my dirt and embarrass me."

Trevor's grin flashed. "Some of that, too." He put up his hands. "Okay. Okay, I'll give it a rest. What do you say when we're done we head down to Chelsea Piers with Lena and the Svelta, the Ukrainian girl?"

Normally that sounded like a night he'd be down for. But dinner at the Vosses' was in two days, and he and Val needed more research time to get to know each other, or whatever it was they were doing. He was not into her. She just wasn't nearly as…standoffish as he'd thought. Yeah, that was it. Whatever it was, no way he was telling Trevor he'd rather hang with some chick he wasn't sure he liked than two hot models. Not gonna happen. "I'm beat, man. I need to crash."

Trevor wasn't fooled, though. "Sure you are."

The knock at her door made the butterflies in Val's lower belly scatter. She had to silently remind herself that they were hanging out to get the details so they could both pull off their tasks. But she was starting to like the guy.

Not that she would date him, but he was fun. He'd started to teach her to take pictures. She could get decent photos for her blog with her phone. She understood lighting and composition, but she'd never used a real SLR. So he was teaching her. He'd even given her an old fifty-millimeter so she could practice.

And she was introducing him to good food at all her little hidden gems in the city. They were becoming friends… sort of. Truth was she had no idea what they were. They'd both made it clear that neither of them was interested. He just wasn't…*that* bad. She sighed. Whatever.

When she yanked open the door, Bennett looked every bit like the sexy models he photographed. White T-shirt, dark jeans, scratched-up boots and curling blond hair in a messy disarray. He braced himself in her doorway, and she took a moment to stare, because good lord, the man was pretty. "How come you were never a model?" The words were out of her mouth before she even consciously registered the thought.

A smile played on his lips as he gave her a cocky nod. "You're starting to like what you see, huh?"

She rolled her eyes. "Really? You honestly can't help yourself, can you?"

When he gave her his full-blown grin, her breath caught, but she was careful to show no emotion. She was not going to join his revolving door. It did not matter how gorgeous he was.

"Nope, I'm incorrigible. At least that's what Trevor's mom always said. So I was thinking, instead of more question and answer, maybe we do something fun. I'll still answer all your questions, but we could go for a ride or something?"

"A ride?"

"Yep. On my bike."

"O-on your bike?"

"Yes," he said slowly, as if she'd lost her mind. "Motorcycle. Come on, it'll be fun."

"I've never been on a motorcycle."

"I figured. You'll need to change. It's not that warm out yet, but jeans are good, you know—casual."

"Actually I have this dining in the dark thing I need to do. Where your whole dining experience is in the dark and most of the waitstaff is blind. There have been a few of these restaurants in the city, but the chef is a friend, so I promised I'd go to opening night."

"Okay, we'll take my bike there. And you can still look dinner appropriate in jeans. Come on. This is all part of the loosening-up plan, remember?"

She was starting to regret telling him that. "Fine, but I will kill you if you get me tossed off or whatever."

"I promise, Miss Valentine Anderson. You're safe with me."

Why was it she didn't believe him?

Chapter 9

"Seriously, though. What was that I ate? I mean, that was incredible." Bennett let Val out of the elevator first. "I need to eat that again."

She laughed and gave him a smile over her shoulder. "I agree. Sometimes you just have to eat duck prepared the right way. It was amazing. I made an appointment with the chef to go by the restaurant and take pictures tomorrow."

"You want me to come with you? I *am* a professional. Free of charge."

Val swallowed hard as warmth spread through her chest. He might be arrogant and a giant pain in the ass, but he could also be sweet, and right about now she was thinking about how he tasted. Which was extremely counterintuitive. "Well, I'm not going to say no to a professional. Even though he has a business to run."

"I don't know if you know this, but I'm kind of a big

deal, remember?" he said with a wink, and she couldn't help but laugh.

"Okay, but I want to try on my own, so maybe you could just guide me?"

"Sure, whatever. I just want to help you get better." He nodded with a big grin.

"Liar. You want more of those duck meatballs." He would have stolen hers, too, if they hadn't been completely in the dark. He'd certainly been reaching for them. Or he'd been reaching to take her hand. But she knew better.

"Well, those *and* the crème brûlée. I mean, good lord, woman, did you taste that?"

"I was there, remember?"

"Yes, but you were doing your superhero thing, so you might not have been enjoying the moment."

"Superhero thing?" she laughed.

"Yeah, your sense of smell and your ability to taste are totally a superpower. We should get you a cape. But you were so focused on the ingredients, I doubt you tasted it just for fun. I'll tell you. It was delicious."

She couldn't help but laugh. She loved it when someone else saw things the way she did. And he was right. She'd been in work mode, using palate cleansers and discerning every little pinch of cilantro and vanilla bean. She hadn't been out for just the fun of it. But it had been fun. And he made great company. Though the bike ride was totally terrifying. Exhilarating, but terrifying. It made everything that much sharper. That much more alive. "I know it was delicious." She stopped in front of her door. "So thank you for the ride."

"How'd you like it?"

"You mean careening around the city with a rocket between my legs?"

He grinned. "I love it when you talk dirty to me."

Despite herself, she laughed. "You really are incorrigible."

"I know." She cleared her throat. "So I guess I'll see you tomorrow night. Anything in particular I should wear?"

His gaze slid down her body, warming her from the inside out. When he spoke his voice was gravelly. "Uh, you look great in whatever you wear."

Oh. Okay, then. She'd have to wait until she got inside to fan herself. Or even better, take a cold shower. All night he'd been feeding her little compliments. It didn't help that they'd been completely in the dark and had had to rely on touching each other to navigate dinner. Rely on brushes, voice, breathing. It was all a slow seduction. And she was wound too tight right now.

She cleared her throat. "At least tell me if they're formal."

Bennett blinked as if she'd dragged him out of his thoughts. "A little black dress will be fine."

"Okay, I'll manage something." With a deep inhale, she said, "Well, good night, Bennett. Tonight was fun."

His gaze dropped to her lips. "It was."

"I'll see you tomorrow for the photos if you're still interested." She unlocked her door and preceded in front of him.

"Oh, I'm interested."

Val wished she had more time to mentally brace herself, but when Bennett leaned close she couldn't move. Not a millimeter. All she wanted were his lips on hers, making her feel alive. Like the ride on his bike.

When he stepped into her space, his whisper was low, harsh. "I have been dying to do this since you opened the door tonight." The tension around them crackled. She could see the war of emotions in his pale eyes. He was fighting something, but she didn't know what. When he crushed his lips to hers, the tension around her exploded.

Bennett paused a second before their lips met and he took the time to catalog everything about this second. Her scent, they way her lips parted, the way she held on to him. Because he knew, the moment their lips touched, he wouldn't remember anything. He wouldn't be able to think straight, and he'd be a goner.

She made the sweetest little gasping sound just before their lips met, and he groaned into the kiss. She tasted of the spice from the sauce. And sweet from the crème brûlée. And her own intoxicating taste. It didn't take long to get lost under her spell. Just a couple of sinfully sweet licks of her tongue and his brain shorted; he couldn't breathe or think or make any sense of his world. All he knew was he couldn't stop.

Her hands clutched his T-shirt and he pulled her close, digging his hands into her hair, then caressing her back, anchoring her body against his. Val's soft, sweet curves molded against him and his body went rigid with the need to possess her. To have her. To call her his.

His erection pulsed against her belly, and all he could hear was the lust-infused blood rushing in his skull. *More. More. More.* The chant echoed in his head, and he gave up any shred of fighting.

In the morning, she might have regrets. She might wish she hadn't done this, but he had known from the second he'd kissed her the first time that they were combustible together.

Like a supercharged accelerant and match, they blew things up, singeing anything in their path before completely eviscerating it.

He lifted her easily and she wrapped her legs around him. Hell, he wanted her in bed. Naked, hot and fast, but there was a part of him that also wanted to savor this passionate, needy, desperate feeling.

When he braced her against the door and took her hands into one of his and held them above her head, she made a little oomph sound. He slid his tongue deep, stroking into her mouth, and she met him thrust for thrust.

But it was when she started to rock her sweet center against the rigid length of him that he lost it. He couldn't think, and all that mattered in the world to him was kissing her. Getting more of *this* with *her*. Making her half as crazy as she was making him.

Bennett dragged his mouth from Val's even as he braced her against the doorway with his hips; she tasted so damn sweet and intoxicating all over.

There was a part of him that could kiss her all night and be perfectly satisfied. Just kissing her was enough to tilt his world off center. The rest of this—touching her—it just dragged him into the abyss of needing this girl. Not that he was complaining.

He nuzzled her throat with his nose while he tucked his hands under her soft cotton shirt. He wanted to take his time. He really did. But her hard, pebbled nipples had been pressing into his back that whole ride. And right now, he just wanted to touch them. Needed to make her call his name.

Damn, she was full, overflowing his hands. When he rolled his thumbs over the stiff peaks, her back bowed and she cried out his name.

"Mmm, that sound is music to my ears," he whispered as he teased her. He sought her mouth again, swallowing her cries of pleasure as he plucked and teased. Her hips kept their steady motion over his erection, and he started to shake. If she kept that up, he was going to—

"Val," he ground out. "What are you doing to me?"

"Bennett, I need…" Her voice trailed as she arched her back again.

"I know. I need you, too." Lifting her away from the door, he carried her to the couch and laid her back against the soft cushions. If there was one thing he knew how to do, it was undress a woman. Her jeans went first, and then he pulled up her top. Problem was, he got side-tracked with her breasts and could only stare as his mouth went completely dry.

"B-Bennett?" She made a move to cover up, but he stayed her hands.

"Please don't cover up. You're beautiful."

Val flushed and ducked her head. "You're staring."

"Yeah, well, have you seen your breasts? I should build a shrine to them and all the things I want to do to them. You want me to tell you?"

She bit her lip even as she nodded slightly.

"Let me show you instead." Bennett had her bra off in seconds. But he wasn't happy until he had one off her dark tips between his lips and licked her, sucking her deep.

Val dug her hands into his hair and tugged, alternating between pulling him closer and tugging him away. "Bennett, oh, God."

He muttered something unintelligible because, hell, he was tasting her, touching her and he couldn't think and she tasted so damn good. He switched breasts, teasing the other with his thumb.

Her soft cries of his name drove him faster even as she parted her thighs to make room for his questing hand as he sucked. Edging her panties aside with his thumb, he inserted a finger into her gently, pressing against that bundle of nerves deep inside. Val broke apart with a low, guttural moan.

He lifted his head to watch her face as she climaxed and reveled in the shock and need plainly etched on her beautiful features. "You are so perfect, just like this."

Her eyes met his, and he knew she understood that he meant more than in just the moment—that she was perfect as she was. She didn't need to change anything, be anyone else. At least he hoped she understood.

You weren't supposed to be falling for her. Yeah, well, it was too late for that, now wasn't it?

As her thighs quaked, he dragged off his T-shirt and made quick work of the rest of their clothes. He pulsed painfully, but when he looked down at her, her dewy slickness calling to him, he wanted to taste her before making love to her. Because once he entered, he'd never want to leave.

As he slid down her body, she tried to sit up. "Bennett? What are you doing?

He smiled up at her. "I'm going to taste you."

Her eyes went wide, and he had to grin at the look of surprise. "Wait, you don't have to. Maybe we—"

He shook his head. "You know what? You are beautiful and smart and funny, but if you're going to say anything along the lines of I don't *have* to, or you think I don't like it, then I'm going to ask you to stop talking now."

She opened her mouth and then closed it again with an audible click of her teeth.

He grinned. "Okay, then. Lie back and let me taste you. Got it?"

A slow smile spread over her lips. "Okay."

His erection pulsed again against his thigh in frustration. *Easy, fella, we'll get to you.* Except he didn't want to stop. With long, leisurely licks at her folds, occasionally pausing to circle around her pleasure button, he kept licking until her thighs quaked around him and she called out his name over and over again on release.

With a smile, he rose up, stopping to kiss his favorite spots along the way. A hip bone here, a belly button there. The oh-so-soft skin on the underside of her breast, the hollow of her throat.

When he rolled away to find his wallet, she reached weakened arms for him. Bennett made quick work of the condom then settled between her splayed legs again. When she met his gaze directly, he knew this was unique. *She* was different. And when he dived into her velvet depths, their bodies melding together, he knew he never wanted to leave.

"Oh, my, Bennett…yes." Val's fingernails dug into his back and he had to fight against the charge of electricity winding its way around his spine as her muscles squeezed him again, holding him prisoner inside her, in an attempt to keep them permanently joined.

Bennett kissed her deep, and when he pulled back, her smile was soft and her eyes widened in wonder. It was then that he knew just how much trouble he was in. There would be no forgetting Valentine Anderson. And with that thought seared into his mind, he let go of control and let the release tumble him over the edge into oblivion.

Chapter 10

Bennett wrapped himself around the woman in bed and gently stroked her nipple with his thumb. God, she smelled so good. She wiggled into his caress and he groaned, his body ready to go again.

Through the night, how many times had they made love? How many times had she called his name on breathy sighs? Well, a few, because she was prone to chanting. He popped his eyes open and squinted at the glare of sunlight streaking across the white duvet. What the hell? It was morning?

He'd slept over? As soon as the question formed, his mind snapped awake as if jammed full of epinephrine. *Valentine. Oh, shit.*

It all came crashing into him. Kissing her at the door. He wasn't sure what the hell had possessed him. But all through dinner, he'd kept thinking about her lips and wanting to taste them again.

He understood the basic rules. One simple one, really—don't sleep with the woman pretending to be your girlfriend.

But she'd been so sweet and they'd been having a great time and next thing he knew, they were kissing and he was lifting her up and carrying her into her apartment.

Just remembering how she tasted made his erection jerk against her butt. She whimpered something about more sleep. *Hell. Hell, hell, hell.* She was his one shot to get this Voss thing right, and he'd screwed it up by sleeping with her.

You're an idiot. Worse, he wanted to do it again. Like last night. They'd made love three times. This was not supposed to happen to him. And he'd spent the night? His sex-fuzzed brain offered up the image of him passing out with her sprawled on top of him.

He'd broken all the rules. First, don't sleep with her. Second, don't spend the night. Third, keep things light. And finally, don't catch a case of feelings.

He scrubbed a hand over his face. Trevor was right. The more time he spent with her, the longer he wanted to keep doing it. And he didn't have time for a relationship. He was heading out soon, if everything went well.

She stirred in the bed, and when she spoke, her voice was hushed and hoarse. "I think the front door offers your best escape hatch. Being six stories up, the window is out."

"I'm not trying to escape."

She rolled over, the sheets clutched to her breasts. "Yes, you are. I usually get up at five. You were holding me pretty tight, so I had no choice but to wait until you were awake. I figured you'd, uh, go home at some point."

"Someone knocked me out." Though now, he was

more than ready and willing to do it again. He needed help. "Val, look—"

"You don't have to give the speech. Where you tell me this was fun but it's not serious and you're busy. Clearly last night we got caught up in the moment. It's not a big deal."

As she spoke his heart hammered against his chest. She was more than cool. Why was she so blasé?

"Val, come on."

"No, I said I wanted to let loose, have fun. And we did that. You don't have to worry. I'm not going to go get your name tattooed on my butt or anything."

"That's a bummer. I could be your tattoo artist."

She laughed. "I really don't do needles. My point is, I had a great time. And you are clearly *very* good. There is a reason women line up outside your door. I'm not going to think you're suddenly in love with me or anything. Nothing has to change about our plans."

His brows shot up. "You still want to move forward?"

She nodded slowly. "If you don't mind. I kind of like being spontaneous. And exciting and slightly irresponsible. You can help me do that."

Oh, hell, what was she saying? Could she see the internal conflict in his eyes? "You want to keep doing *this*? Last night?"

She licked her lips. "Yeah, I guess I do. Temporarily, of course. Clearly we, uh, work well together. After this is over, we'll stop. I'm trying something new. And while we might not have been able to keep our hormones in check, I like how it feels being a little out of control."

He slid down to pull her close. "So, what, we're friends with the best kinds of benefits now?"

"Look at you wanting to label things."

He had to smile at that as he brushed a lock of hair off

her shoulder. "Okay. In that case, there is another benefit I want to try." Even as he kissed her again, he tried to shove aside the twinge of regret. He wasn't a relationship guy. This was the best of both worlds. And she clearly she felt the same.

Chapter 11

"It's lovely to have you over, Valentine. When Adriana told me Bennett had a fiancée, I couldn't have been more thrilled."

"Thank you. Your home is beautiful." And Val wasn't lying. Even if Adriana Voss was after Bennett, Val couldn't fault her taste. The Voss penthouse overlooked Central Park and the wash of natural light made the already open space seem cavernous. Adriana's choices might have been a little bland in the color department for Val, but from the textures to the paintings on the wall, it was perfect.

"Thank you. Adriana did all that." Milton Voss studied her closely. "Ever since she mentioned you, I was very curious to meet the woman who took Bennett Cooper off the market."

She ducked her head and glanced at Bennett where he sat stiffly on the couch trying to hold a conversation with Adriana, who was sitting far too close. She spoke just a little louder to bring Bennett into the discussion. "Would you believe when I first met him, I didn't like him at all? But over time I saw how great he is."

Bennett grinned at her, taking the opportunity to get up. "Well, I grew on you."

"Like a fungus," she muttered and he laughed, draping an arm around her shoulder and kissing her cheek.

Voss smiled at the two of them. "Ah, young love. I remember those days. When you can't keep your hands off each other. It's fantastic."

"Well, Val is fantastic. I don't know where I'd be if she never said yes to me."

The note of sincerity in his voice made her heart pinch. Yes, that part was the truth. And she understood what it meant, even if Voss assumed Bennett meant his proposal.

Adriana stood and wandered over to them. "Given his reputation, you must be some woman." The emphasis on *woman* made Val think Adriana had meant to use another word entirely.

"She is."

Val squirmed. If Bennett kept rubbing circles into her side with his thumb, Val might not be responsible for her actions. She was pretty sure he was turning her on on purpose. *Jackass.* "Thank you, baby. Bennett appeals to my adventurous side."

Adriana Voss narrowed her gaze. "Well, I must say, dear, you're not his usual type. I know Bennett has dated *a lot* of models." Before Bennett could interrupt she said, "If the rumors are true, of course. He's been such the bad boy. I guess you've reformed him from his naughty ways."

Val caught the ticking in Bennett's jaw before he

spoke. "Don't believe everything you read in the papers. When I'm committed to something, I'm all in."

Adriana placed a hand on Bennett's arm and Val had to struggle not to toss it off. "Oh, dear, you mustn't take that the wrong way. I just know it can be challenging for a new couple when the other is traveling all the time. I mean, look at me and Milton. We were hot and heavy, too, but our work keeps us apart for so long. We have to try hard to make it work whatever way possible. You two have certainly found a solution."

What Adriana Voss didn't know was Val had been dealing with nuanced insults all her life. Her mother was an expert, so she wasn't fazed by anything this woman could say. "That we have. I'm so excited to take this man to the altar with me. I know we have a lifetime of laughter and love ahead of us."

The older woman's smile morphed into a scowl as her brows drew down. "Well, of course. Whatever magic spell you cast on him, I wish you well. If the rumors are true, Bennett, you've never had an exclusive relationship, right? Valentine must be truly special, like her name suggests."

Bennett's voice was low as he spoke. "She *is* special. Completely unlike anyone I've ever been with. And that's what I needed. Someone different so I could see what I've been missing. To her my past doesn't matter."

Before Adriana could start again, they were called in for dinner. Val slowed her pace. "You okay?" she asked quietly.

He shook his head. "Yeah. I just hate having to do this."

"Well, it'll be over soon. I promise." More than wanting to put Adriana in her place, there was no way she was standing by and letting her maul Bennett.

Careful there, princess, your feelings are showing. But for right now he was hers.

Back in his apartment, Bennett couldn't lift his dour mood. For the most part, he couldn't care less about his reputation. Nobody knew the real him. But to have Val subjected to it from Adriana, and in his own way, Voss— none of it gave him the warm fuzzies.

Val, however, deflected, reworded, defended. With aplomb and grace, she protected him. It was far more than he had ever asked for. For the most part he could take it. Whatever. The only reputation he cared about was his ability to get the job done. And on that level, he was a bona fide rock star. He turned down more jobs than he could possibly do in a year. *Then why does it feel so empty?*

The real bomb to his need had happened later in the evening as they were leaving Voss's house. He'd seen it. In the study, there was a photo of a snow fox cub, all alone and mewling for its mama. He knew the image well. It was one of his father's.

There were days when he missed his parents so much it hurt almost as much as the day they'd died. And other days where he could almost forget that they were gone. Those days were the worst. The ones when he didn't think about them. It felt like he should think about them more than he did. Would they be proud of him? *Probably not.*

The door to his apartment opened, and he knew without turning it was Val.

She'd gone home to change when they returned to the loft.

He knew he was messing this up. On all fronts. She was sweet. And the more he got to know her, the more he saw just how unpretentious and kind she was. She kept herself closed off because she was afraid of the perception. But once she opened up, she was bright, chatty and fun. She was silly, and being with her was effortless.

Tonight, as Adriana tried to make her crack, everything slid off her like she was Teflon. It pissed him off to no end when she said she'd dealt with worse than Adriana. Had she learned to brush off insults like that because of her mother? He gritted his teeth at the thought.

You are so screwed.

He was totally falling for her. Somewhere in the midst of him learning about her, she'd started to slip past his defenses. He didn't like it, because he didn't want to be one more person who hurt her.

"You okay? You've been really quiet since we left. Don't let the shit Adriana says get to you. Now she should leave you the hell alone. Mission accomplished. She pushes the issue again, I will be a lot less polite."

"It's not her I'm worried about. It's that none of what she said was a lie. The reputation. My partying. I don't look too closely most of the time, but I can't help but wonder if my parents would have been disappointed in me. All I wanted to do was be like them. I idolized my father. I swear I can see him sometimes shaking his head at me. Like, 'son, what the hell are you doing?'"

"I'm sure they loved you."

He shook his head. "I know that. I just can't help thinking I should be doing more to live up to their legacy."

"This is your life. Isn't that what you told me the other day? You determine what you want to keep and what to throw away. You don't like something, you have the power to change it. To be something else. Be someone else. You don't have to be *this*."

"I'm used to going it alone. I've been a selfish prick

for so long. I thought I just liked my life like that. Turns out it's a great way to keep people away."

"Well, you're stuck with me. When this is over, I think we'll be good friends. Now that I know you're not a motorcycle club drug runner or something. We could even work together sometimes. It'll be great. I made a friend out of this whole ordeal. You saved me from myself. From James. To think I wanted to be with that guy." She shook her head.

The problem was, he was starting to think he wanted to be a lot more than friends. And he had no idea what to do about it.

She shifted on her bare feet, her sweatpants brushing against the floor. She looked so tiny and innocent and he wanted to protect her from the Jameses of the world— and from himself. "You're pretty great, you know that?"

Val knew what she'd told him, that they could do this whole casual thing. But the truth was, there was nothing nonchalant about her, and she was getting attached. She was already too involved. She cared about him and seeing him hurting worried her. But she wasn't going to tell him that. Instead, she was just going to pretend she could do this. That they could be friends.

She was drinking her own Kool-Aid. She'd been a fool to think this could stop at any time. Maybe she wasn't too far gone.

When Bennett looked at her like that, with eyes soft, lips tilted into a lopsided grin, muscles all bunched and tight, her brain took a vacation and her heart tried to convince her that this was real. That she belonged in his arms.

She gently touched his back, letting her fingers play

over his bunched muscles, and took pride in the way they twitched under her touch.

When he turned she thought maybe making love again would be more of the same. That frenzied, desperate, clawing need to be together like last time. But no. He was gentle, achingly tender. His kisses lingered. His gaze stayed on hers, intense but with something else laced through it. Something softer, something more emotional. Something like love.

No, Val, don't believe it. This is just a friends thing. You are not to fall in love with the rolling stone.

Yeah, well, someone should tell her heart that.

When he carried her into his bedroom at the top of the loft and stripped off her clothing, taking the time to kiss all of his favorite parts more than once, she shivered in his arms, longing to stay there forever.

As he teased her nipple, making her breath catch, and her back arched and her legs splayed to make room for him. In her mind, she tried to catalog every piece of this experience.

Because one day soon, when the wedding was done and this was all over, she wouldn't have this anymore. She wouldn't know what it was like to be loved like this.

It's not love.

Maybe not, but she could pretend. And even if it wasn't the real deal, she understood how she should be cared for. How she should be treated. She wasn't going back to before. She wasn't going back to less than she deserved.

But as he loved her, there was a point when something shifted. Where everything turned from *Don't get too attached* to *What if this was real? What if he could love you?*

Because the way Bennett studied her as he rocked into her looked a lot like love. He kissed her deep and whispered her name even as his body took hers, rolling them both over so she sat astride him. He worshipped her with his eyes and hands. She knew something in his gaze was different. Val clamped her thighs over his, desperate to hold on to that emotion in his eyes that she couldn't quite place. And as her orgasm rolled over her, sending her to her happiest places, she knew she'd fallen in love with Bennett Cooper. She could only hope that he might love her back.

Chapter 12

This time when Bennett woke up, he knew just where he was. Somewhere in the last two weeks, he'd fallen for the woman with the dark eyes, wide smile and unholy love of flavor.

And that reality scared the hell out of him. Val was the complete opposite of everyone he'd ever been with. Polar opposite to what he'd always told himself he wanted. But now what he wanted was to keep on holding her. To let her past the wall. Let her *see* him. The real him. And if she didn't like what she saw? She might embrace all of it. But she'd been genuine when she said they would actually be friends after all this.

And she was deluded as hell if she thought he could give her up now. Maybe he needed to show her how it could be. All she'd seen of him so far was the carefree, fun guy, and she enjoyed him. Maybe she'd keep him around if he was a little more emotionally open.

Bennett slid his gaze over her sleeping form. Two weeks ago, the idea of a woman in his bed would have had him running for the hills. His bed was *his* space. But he relished having Val here. He wanted her to stay here.

Her lashes fluttered lightly as her eyes scanned back and forth with the frenetic energy of REM sleep. Easing out of bed, he stretched and yawned. When was the last time he'd been so relaxed? She had a calming effect on him, that was for sure. The fire still burned. But it wasn't so frantic.

After throwing on boxers, he padded into the kitchen. He might be questionable with anything dinner related, but pancakes he could do. His mom had taught him. As he pulled out the stuff for the batter and dragged out his frying pan, his phone buzzed on the counter. "Yeah, hello?"

"Bennett? It's Milton."

"Mr. Voss. Hello." He took one glance at the clock. Hell, it was barely eight in the morning. "What can I do for you?"

"Well, it seems that the original photography team for *Earth*'s expedition to Antarctica has run into an issue. The lead photographer has an Argentine visa problem. Would you like to go in his place?"

Bennett froze. "A-Antarctica. You're serious?" This would be an opportunity to showcase his talent. For years he'd been chasing his father's legacy. This would be a chance to prove himself.

"That I am. You would leave in two weeks, on the twenty-first. You'll be gone for a month. You think that pretty fiancée of yours will survive that long without you?"

He'd be leaving Val behind. Automatically his gaze swung to the loft where she still slept. He cared about her. He could have both. He'd just have to figure it out. "Yes, she'll be fine. I want this."

"Fantastic. I'll have Clair call you with details."

"Thank you, sir."

When he hung up with Voss, Bennett leaned against the counter. Wow. He was getting his dream. Finally. This was his chance. This was something his father would be proud of. Something good that he'd be doing. He'd worked so hard to get here. Newfound feelings or not, he had to take advantage of the opportunity. He and Val would work it out.

He just had to prove that he was the kind of man she wanted to be with.

Val's nose twitched and she peeled open one eyelid. The harsh sunlight directly in her eyes made her groan, and she burrowed under the covers. Instinctively she reached for Bennett to use him as a shield. He was bigger. If they spooned, he would block out the sun.

Except his side of the bed was cold. She patted around and eventually sat up and rubbed her eyes. The smell of coffee snapped her synapses into focus. She heard clanging around in the kitchen and part of her was a little afraid to venture down there. He'd said he was a disaster in the kitchen. Well, no, he'd been dinner specific. Strange thing was, all of it smelled *good*.

She scooted out of bed, dragging the sheet with her as she searched for her sweats. He'd taken them off her downstairs, probably on purpose, knowing she'd have to come down naked to retrieve them. The man was diabolical. Despite that, a smile tugged at the corners of her lips until she noticed the framed newspaper clipping on the dresser.

She stood and wrapped the sheet sarong-style. The

clipping included a photo of a little boy and two adults. Presumably his parents. The caption read, "Billionaire Vincent Cooper, photographed here with his wife, Lily, and their son, Bennett, before their round-the-world expedition."

They looked so happy, and the love was clear and apparent as the little boy looked up at his parents adoringly.

Tears stung her eyes as her heart broke into pieces. That poor little boy. How alone must he have been. He couldn't be older than nine or so in the picture.

"We hit a squall near Panama. They shoved me on a survivor raft and told me to hang on for help when the boat capsized. Both of them were strong swimmers, but the water was just too rough."

Val whirled around. "Oh, my God, Bennett. I'm so sorry."

He put the tray down on the bedside table. "I keep that picture because it's the last recorded memory of how happy we were. I was so excited to get to go with them. Dad made money in tech early. Twentysomething wunderkind. In his thirties, he sold his company to do photography full-time. That picture in Voss's study—that was one of his."

She sucked in a sharp breath. "That's why you were so upset last night."

He nodded. "He and my mom. They were great. They weren't perfect, but I loved them so much. I—" He dragged in a deep breath. "I don't tell anyone who I am. The kind of women I've been with, they're different from you—they see dollar signs or they pity me or something. So I've never gotten close to anyone. Well, except Trevor."

"You thought you couldn't tell me? I'm not some random girl. I wouldn't have looked at you any differently."

He had a point, though. They didn't really know each other. It had only been a couple of weeks. Never mind that she already felt closer to him than anyone save Mel.

"I know. It's a habit. A bad one. The only reason Trevor makes it past is he doesn't let up. After my parents were gone, I was sent to my aunt's in New York. Trevor was my neighbor. I swear, the kid showed up every day to ask if I would play. Every day for six months before I would even talk to him. I was a pretty stubborn kid."

"Was?"

A light smile played on his lips. "Okay, am."

Val wanted to hug him, wanted to hold that little boy and tell him it would be okay. She wanted to hug the man and tell him that he could tell her things. But she had no idea how. Tapping into her emotional stores wasn't something she ever allowed herself to do. "Bennett, what I said last night. It still stands. They would be so proud of you."

He shook his head. "Not if I keep avoiding." He ran his hands through his hair. "I know a few weeks ago, I told you that you were hiding, and maybe you were, but the truth is, I've been doing the same. I put the mask on and I act. But I don't want to pretend anymore. I want to be real. I want to let people past the brick wall. I want you."

Her? He wanted her? "What are you saying?"

"I'm saying that I'm terrible at this. I've never had a real relationship. I cut and run, that's my MO, but maybe we could be more than just friendly neighbors once this is over. Maybe we could be…more."

More? He wanted more from her? "Are you sure, Bennett? I'm not real good with showing my emotions, either. And you photograph beautiful women for a living. I'm not *that* secure."

He tugged her close. "I'm falling for you. Even after a lifetime of chasing models around for a good photo.

You're the one I want to hold, kiss, touch. How about we try it? All I know is I want to keep waking up to you. Even after your sister's wedding. I'm asking for a shot."

And she wanted to give it to him. But that realization scared her. She'd been hurt too many times. "I want to try, too, but, Bennett, anytime you don't want to do this anymore, don't just vanish on me, please. Just tell me and we'll go back to being friends or neighbors or whatever."

His jaw clenched as he nodded. "Okay. I promise. Right now I just want to hold you. That okay?"

She nodded as she snuggled into his chest and prayed she'd be able to keep from getting hurt.

He whispered into her hair, "So is now a good time to tell you Voss is sending me to Antarctica for a month?"

"Oh?"

"Yeah, he called when you were asleep. For once my photographs will cover something serious. The effects of global warming on our natural landscape. I've done wildlife before, but nothing like this."

"It sounds like this is the perfect opportunity."

Val held him tight so he couldn't see the concern on her face. Not about Antarctica. Or even him. Could she stand it when he finally left?

Chapter 13

Bennett laughed as he checked his text from Val. She'd taken to sending him food porn. First she'd send a text with the hint of something delicious mostly covered with a napkin. The next would be the full meal, completely exposed. She'd even started to give the concoctions outrageously suggestive names. The dessert from the chef she was seeing this morning looked like some kind of orange pudding with a pomegranate seed in the center, then curls of chocolate drawn from the center.

I call this one the hairy nipple.

Bennett snorted, then muffled it when everyone at the shoot turned to stare at him. Trevor eyed him from a corner as the makeup team retouched him. When he lifted a brow, Bennett ignored him.

His friend hadn't let it rest that he'd been right about

Val. He and Bennett had made plans next week to grab a drink so that the two people in his life could get to know each other. But first Bennett had to pass the test with Val's parents tomorrow.

Before it was going to be a whatever thing. Show up. Outrage them a little. Go home. No big deal. Now that he was actually interested in their daughter, he was worried. Yeah, Val didn't see them much and she'd warned him about them, but they were still her parents. And he'd never done the parental thing before. Ever. He wanted them to like him. If for no other reason than it made things easier on her. He texted her back.

I have an idea. How about you text me a real nipple? Far more interesting.

Her response was instant.

With cloud technology? I'm no fool. The only pictures I'll do nude are ones you take on film.

Oh, hell. He stood straight.

You'd let me photograph you?

While he waited, his heart slammed against his ribs. And his breathing shallowed. Because right now, all he could think about was the kind of lighting he would use. He could do a whole series on her titled *My Valentine.* The idea formed, rooting in his brain. Forming branches. *His* Valentine.

Yes. I trust you to make it tasteful.

Oh, it would be tasteful, all right. He didn't want anyone getting too good a look at what he considered his. But he could make it work.

You're giving a man ideas.

Good. Now get back to work. You have real hairy nipples to photograph.

He barked out a laugh and replied.

Nah, they would for sure wax Trevor's chest, but I'll tell him you said so.

When he returned to set, Trevor was smirking. "So, all that laughing. Let me guess. Your girlfriend?"

Heat crept up Bennett's neck. "Man, shut up."

"Nah, it's cool, bro. I mean, the woman has got you on lock, grinning like an idiot. I'm happy for you." He shrugged. "I'll need to take your player card, but I'm happy for you. Just so you know. Player no more."

Player no more. The old him would have fought to hold on to that. But he didn't care about that anymore. "You can tease me all you want. She's pretty damn awesome, so I don't care."

His friend beamed at him. "Even if I'm losing my wingman, I couldn't be happier."

"Yeah, me, too." Though as he worked, a shadow of unease breezed over his skin, giving him goose bumps. Things were going great, but he hadn't forgotten that she hadn't been nearly as enthused as he was to jump in. She was cautious. *Because she knows what's good for her.* He shoved the thought to the back of his mind. Being with him wasn't a risk and he'd show her that. After all, it had been two weeks and he was showing her he was all in. Tomorrow he'd charm the hell out of her parents. It would be fine. He'd barely handed his camera off to his assistant when his phone rang. Anticipating Val, he answered, "Boyfriend extraordinaire at your service."

The voice on the line, however, was not Val's. It was far too deep and familiar for that. "Don't you mean fiancé?"

Milton. Shit. "Mr. Voss. Nice to hear from you. Sorry, I though you were Val."

The older man laughed. "Not a problem, son. But you might want to keep reminding that lovely girl that you're her fiancé now that you've tied her down. A girl that beautiful might think she has free range of motion."

That unease he'd shoved aside was back with a vengeance, casting a dark cloud over his earlier happy mood. "Yeah, working on that. It's all so new. What can I do for you?"

"Well, I was thinking, after the other night, that you'll be off the market soon enough, and you and I haven't spent much time together to get to know each other. So, we could kill two birds with one stone."

"Uh, how's that, sir?"

"Well, you can start by calling me Milton. But then I was thinking we could go out on the town. You could pass off some of your hot girl mojo on to an old man. Strictly for fun."

The unease took hold of every nerve and made Bennett's hairs stand on end. "Sir. Uh, Adriana?"

"My wife and I have an arrangement. And you aren't married yet. So what do you say? Tonight? I'll send the limousine for you."

Tonight? Hell, the rehearsal was tomorrow, followed by brunch. He couldn't tie one on. "Okay, sir, but I do have plans tomorrow. Meeting the in-laws, so not too late."

"Sure, son, sure. We'll be talking a lot about Antarctica. All the details aren't ironed out yet. Nothing's really set in stone you know. I want to make sure you're a good fit. You can be a team player, can't you, Benny?"

Bennett swallowed hard. In other words, "Do as I say or you're off the expedition."

"Yes, sir. I can be a team player." As he hung up, Bennett had a bad feeling that before the night was over he'd have to choose between his two divergent futures.

This was a mistake.
Bennett glared at the shot glass in front of him and wished he'd never agreed to come out. Trevor was supposed to come, too, but he was running late.

But at least Milton was having fun. Two blondes strutted by giving Bennett the eye, but he wasn't biting. They were beautiful, but plastic. Everything about them from their fake enhancements to the platinum hair to the lashes—there was nothing real about them. He could tell from a mile away.

Now that he had something real, he saw them for what they were. They were empty happiness. A few weeks ago he'd have gladly taken one or both home, or rather headed to their place and been out before dawn broke. He used to think that was living.

"What's the matter? You don't look like you're in a celebratory mood, Benny."

"Bennett, sir. Or Ben."

Milton waved a hand dismissively. "Come on, relax. We're here to have fun. What's the matter, you don't like blondes? Given Val, maybe they're not your type. Let's head to the other bar downstairs. Maybe we'll find you someone you like."

He sighed. Milton Voss wanted the Bennett Cooper experience. Too bad *that* Bennett Cooper was on hiatus. Maybe for good. "No, thanks. Like I said, I have somewhere to be in the morning. And I'm with Val."

Voss rolled his eyes. "You're serious about that? She's a nice girl, but one woman for the rest of your life?"

Bennett blinked. "Sir, you're married, right? Adriana's a...beautiful woman." He chose his words carefully.

"Adriana and I have an *arrangement*. As long as we're discreet, we can do as we like. Who better to give me the debauchery tour than the Bennett Cooper?"

Well. That explained a few things. No wonder Adriana didn't give a damn about chasing him. Bennett tried to think of how he'd feel if Val wanted to screw other guys. The rage sparked to life in an instant, and he could easily have punched someone. That didn't suit him. "Well, I'm glad that works for you. Not my thing. I'm with Val."

Voss laughed. "Well, more for me. At least drink with your boss. Then you can go home and do the devoted fiancé thing."

Bennett stared at the shot of top-shelf tequila. All he wanted to do was go home. But Milton Voss was changing his life. The least he could do was have a drink with him. Just the one. For once he wanted to keep a commitment to someone. And he wasn't going to screw this up. Not when Val needed him.

Chapter 14

Val paced as she checked her watch.

Damn. She knew she should have stayed home yesterday so the two of them could drive down together. Instead he'd said he had to deal with Voss and she should go ahead. But it was almost nine thirty and he still wasn't here. *Come on, Bennett. Not today. Today I need you.* But as she stared down the long drive of the church, there was no sign of a cab or an Uber. Or hell, even his bike.

He wasn't coming. Disappointment curled in her chest and she couldn't drag in a breath. Everything had been great with them. Fine. *This is just like Marcus.*

"Honestly, we need to keep everything on schedule. Your little date isn't coming, Valentine."

Her mother's voice broke her out of her spiral. "He's coming, Mom." He'd promised. "He's definitely coming." At least she prayed he was.

Her father came out of the heavy oak doors. "What's

the holdup? At this rate we'll miss our reservation if we don't get going. Come on, you two."

"Your daughter is waiting for her new boyfriend."

Her father rolled his eyes. "Honestly, Valentine. Your mother told me about this new guy. A photographer, really? You are the daughter of professors, and that's who you pick? We'll discuss it later. Come on, he can meet you inside. Your sister is waiting. This is her time to shine, not yours."

Ouch. Way to toss that zinger, Dad.

Her mother tried to tug her inside. "Honestly, instead of someone like James, you're wasting your time on this boy. James is the chupacabra. A strong black man. He's good-looking and connected."

"He's Ned Flanders, Mom."

Her mother frowned. "Who?"

"Never mind. Bennett is great and—"

"If he's so great, where is he?"

Just then the crunch of gravel under tires had her turning and her heart soared. "That's him." She tore her arm from her mother's grasp and ran down the stairs. Her parents left her to it and went back inside. "Oh, my God, where have—"

But Bennett wasn't the only one to climb out of the cab. Trevor was with him. "Val, I'm sorry."

The moment Bennett spoke, Val had to step backward. The alcohol stench practically smacked her in the face. "Are you drunk right now?"

He weaved and Trevor held him up. "Val. It's not what it looks like." His words were so slurred she could barely understand him.

Trevor stepped in. "Look, I know, but he didn't do this on purpose. Voss made him come out last night. It was like forced hazing or some shit."

Val stared at the two of them. "You seem fine."

"Yeah, but that's because I showed up late and asked the bartender to make my drinks nonalcoholic. Voss was in the mood to misbehave, and he insisted Bennett was the one to take him down that path."

"I can't even right now." She glared at the two of them.

Bennett reached for her, stumbling out of Trevor's grasp. "Val. Wait. I'm sorry. I wanted to be fear…" He cleared his throat. "Here. *Be here*. I wanted to be here."

"So you do this. You said it was *a* drink. I needed you."

Trevor inclined his head. "I'll just…be over here." He moved a few feet away and occupied himself with his phone.

"I'll make it up to you. It's fine. I'm here now." He reached for her.

"You're here, but you're *drunk*."

He spread his arms. "But, hey, I showed up. You should count your lucky stars. I could have been a no-show."

She glared at him. "Are you serious right now?"

He scrubbed a hand down his face. "I'm sorry. I'm sorry. I'm screwing this up. I'm so drunk and I wanted to be here for you. You trusted me. Best thing that's ever happened to me. I swear." Except *swear* came out as *shear*.

"Bennett. I don't even know what—"

The doors to the church opened. "Seriously, Val, you're doing this at my wedding rehearsal? I mean, I know you're not in the wedding party, but you're my sis—"

Solstice stopped when she saw Bennett and Trevor. "Oh, is this him? The *magical* boyfriend?" She put a hand up under her nose. "My nose isn't as sensitive as yours, but even I can tell he smells like a bar. Seriously, Val?"

"Sol, just go inside, I'll be right there."

"Not with him you won't." She squinted. "Wait, he looks familiar." Her attention was trained on Bennett. Pulling out her phone, she laughed. "Oh, wow. You're Bennett Cooper, the photographer?"

He nodded and swayed. "Congratulations. Sorry I'm so drunk."

Sol held out her phone to Val. "This is the guy you're holding up my rehearsal for?"

Val stared down at a video from TMZ on Sol's phone. A photographer asked Bennett, "How is the man about town now? You've been quiet lately. Rumor is you're locked up."

Bennett shook his head. "Nope. Single Bennett Cooper. Always single. Always alone. Besides, I always screw up. Who would put up with me?"

Val stared and fought the nausea. *Single.* "You're single, huh?"

Sol frowned. "I thought you were together. Serious and all that." Her sister narrowed her gaze. "Or did you make that up? Oh, Val, how pathetic is that?"

Bennett shook his head. "No. Wait. Val. *And* Solstice. What kind of name is Solstice, anyway? Whatever. I can explain. We're together. I want—"

Val shook her head. "No. Don't bother. I'm going inside. You can go."

She'd made a mistake. This was what trying to step out of her box got her. *Heartbroken.* She might be falling in love with him. But he didn't feel the same, that much was clear.

"Val."

"Bennett, just go. I'm tired."

She didn't look back at him as she followed her sister inside.

Chapter 15

"I messed up, Trev." Bennett's head felt like it would pop off if he even tried to lift it. The hangover from last Friday had taken two days to dissipate. And then he'd spent the next week trying to get Val to talk to him. But she'd gone stone silent. Either she wasn't staying at her place or she was real good at avoiding answering the door. He had to work, so she could have slipped in and out while he was gone. But more than likely she was staying with a friend.

And then, like a moron, he'd brought out the eighteen-year-old scotch and tried to bury the aching hole in his chest. *Smart move.*

"Yeah, you did, but you don't need me to tell you that."

"Aren't you supposed to help me?"

"Sure. I am helping you. I'm telling you the truth. You screwed up bad. I'm just waiting for you to tell me how the hell you plan on fixing it."

"I've tried. I've tried, man. I leave in two days. I don't want to just let it go."

"Then do something. Don't do the Bennett thing where you just let it dissolve. Where you just back away, erect a wall. She's good for you. You need to do something to repair this."

"But how? She won't talk to me."

"Okay, then you'll go to Antarctica for a month. And while you're gone, somebody else will snatch her up. You keep sitting on your ass."

Despite the raging headache, Bennett pushed himself to sitting. "The hell they will."

Trevor nodded. "This is more like it. I like seeing you fired up. Now what are you going to do?"

"I leave in two days, the day of the wedding. I can try and see her there."

Trevor nodded. "That's more like it. Except what are you going to do if she doesn't want to see you?"

"I will grovel if I have to. I love the girl."

His friend grinned. "See, now, was that so hard to say?"

Bennett rubbed the aching center of his chest. "Yes, but I'm going to keep saying it until she hears me."

"Awesome. And no more self-sabotage?"

"What are you talking about? I wasn't sabotaging myself."

"Seriously, dude?"

"Voss wanted—"

Trevor crossed his arms over his chest. "For real?"

"Fine. I could have stopped at two and insisted. But I want this gig. I *need* it. It's what I've been working toward all this time."

"This had nothing to do with that. Voss and his wife are messing with you. Maybe her more than him. But you can distance yourself from them. You want this job, but there will be others. You show how good you are. What you can do. You get to dictate your terms."

Bennett forced himself into a standing position. First things first. He was taking a shower. The way he smelled, he wasn't going near her like this. Her nose would go crazy. It was time to pull his life together. If he wanted her, he was going to have to fight. Because she deserved that much from him. "You're right. I'm on it. I'm going to that wedding."

"As if I've ever been wrong. Maybe that one time in '96."

Bennett rolled his eyes. "Hey, Trev."

His friend looked up from his phone. "Yeah, man?"

"Thanks for the pep talk."

The other man shrugged. "It's nothin'. I like what she does to you. You become the more open version of yourself, so that's cool. Besides, I didn't want to have to deal with your morose ass when you get back from penguin country."

Bennett laughed. "Got you." Now all he had to do was win Valentine back. He just wished he had a clue how to do that.

Chapter 16

This was a mistake.

Val shifted in her seat and tried to focus in front of her instead of on her phone in her purse. *You could call him. He might still come. Call him.*

No. Hell, no. She was *not* calling Bennett. Never mind that she hadn't had a decent night's sleep since last Saturday. She'd thought she could stay home, but as she spent more than an hour listening for his footsteps, she knew that was a bad idea. Instead, she'd packed up and gone to Mel's. It was closer for the wedding, anyway. She wasn't an idiot—she would have to go home eventually. But she just needed some time to separate and not obsess.

Except she'd just obsessed at Mel's instead of at home.

Bennett hadn't called. He hadn't texted. A part of her had thought he might, but then she reminded herself of the nature of their brief relationship. She'd helped him out. He was supposed to help her out. But that hadn't worked out how she'd planned. And after the embarrassment of her parents finding out they weren't really together, she had to endure her mother's pity setups. Her mother had called James, who'd agreed to come with her. Heaven forbid the seating plans be all messed up.

"You can at least say thank you."

Val forced herself to sit perfectly still. She was pretty sure whacking James on the head with her shoe would ruin her sister's day. Especially if she used the pointy four-inch heel. "You seem to forget that you were trying to dump me. And you were doing a bad job of it."

"Yeah, but if I'd known that there was some sort of competition, I would have reevaluated my position."

She clenched her jaw. To hell with Sol's wedding. She was going to kill him regardless. "Why did you come, James? It's not like you want to be here."

"On the contrary. I spoke to my father, and he helped me see how you and I together could be a good match."

She rolled her eyes. "Do you even like me? Like, as a person?"

"Of course I like you. You're beautiful, and pleasant enough, unless you're complaining about the smell somewhere. You're smart. Though, unless you're going to go into finance if we stay together, it's probably best you don't work. I do have some political aspirations, and the woman I will need by my side has to aim for something more than lifestyle blogger."

She stared at him for a moment. Was this really her life? At a wedding she didn't want to be at, sitting next to a man she didn't want to date, trying to please a mother who would never be satisfied?

You're not happy.

No. She wasn't. Over the last month, she'd been happy with Bennett. But after what he'd said to that tabloid reporter, could she go back to him? He didn't want to be with her. And wasn't that the whole point of her year of living dangerously? To be out of her comfort zone. To take risks. To find her bliss. This, right here, wasn't giving her any satisfaction. Here, sitting in the hard pew in a dress her mother had squeezed her into, brought zero joy.

And even if Bennett wasn't her future, she deserved to be doing something else. *With* someone else. Because from now on she was going to do things that made her excited.

She turned to James. "You're a poor facsimile for Marcus. He was this guy that broke up with me in college. I thought he was perfect. He went to the right school. Was in the right fraternity. He graduated magna cum laude. Was headed to Yale for law school. And then one day he decided he was done with me and ghosted me. Just pretended I no longer existed."

He frowned. "I don't understand what that has to do with me."

"It has nothing to do with you. It has to do with me. I've been trying to fix that relationship for so long. Trying to get a do-over on what I might have done wrong. I realize now I didn't do anything. Because he dumped me when I spread my wings. I should have taken the cue that he was wrong for me. But no. I'm slow on the uptake. You and I are done. We're not doing this. I'm leaving after the ceremony."

"You're walking away from me?" He blinked as if he couldn't fathom the possibility.

"Yep. Again."

"For that photographer?"

She smiled. "No. Not even. I wish. I love him and I miss him. But even if he and I are done, it still stands. You bring me zero happiness. Matter of fact, you are a joy sucker. I deserve to be the best me. Weird oddities and all. So you might as well go. I won't be needing you to do me any favors."

"You can't imagine how happy that makes me to hear that."

Val whirled in the pew to find Bennett leaning over the next row. "Bennett?"

"Hi, beautiful. I'm so sorry I'm late."

"What are you doing here?"

He stood, looking incredible in his charcoal suit. This was a version of him she'd never seen. He scooted around the guests and marched over to her in full view of everyone. Several of the guests started to whisper. "I'm here to apologize. I'm here to tell you I screwed up. But if you let me, I'll make it up to you."

The air whooshed out of her lungs. "Bennett—"

"Wait." He held up a hand. "Before you tell me all the reasons we don't belong together, hear me out."

The doors opened with an echo, and in her peripheral vision, she saw her mother approaching quickly. "I don't—"

"I'm in love with you. That's the fact. And it scares me. It's terrifying, really. Love. It's far easier to block every emotion out. The problem is you don't truly live like that." With his gaze on hers, he ignored her mother's attempts to grasp his arm. "Mrs. Anderson, I appreciate it's Solstice's wedding, but if you'll just let me profess my love to your other daughter, then we can get this show on the road."

Val tried to hide the giggle, but it escaped anyway. She stood. "Mother, enough. For once in your life, you will put me first. I deserve as much love and respect as you give Sol, and you're going to give it to me. Now, if you'll back off for a minute, I'm trying to listen to Bennett. I'll only be a second. Then Sol can get married."

Her mother's eyes went wide. "How dare you speak to me like—"

Sometime during the power struggle, her father had come down the aisle. He tugged on her mother's arm. "Sweetheart, enough. Val deserves to be happy. Give her a moment with her young man."

Her mother looked like she might argue, but she backed off.

Bennett breathed a sigh of relief. "I'm leaving for my flight to Antarctica in a few hours. I want you to come with me. It's a month away so it won't be the most ideal vacation in the world. But afterward, we can explore South America and all the food. Come with me, please. I need you."

The resident fear tried to cover her like a shroud. Tried to prevent her from saying what she needed. But after one glance at her father, then James, she slid her glance back to Bennett. "I love you. I've missed you."

"Thank God. I know I was an idiot. I wanted to sabotage things because, well, I was terrified you'd leave once you knew me."

"You're not shaking me now. My boyfriend has turned me into someone wild and adventurous."

His smile was broad. As she reached for his hand, he said, "I like the sound of adventurous. Tell me, Valentine Anderson, how flexible are you?"

Val just shook her head. "James, you've been supplanted. Get up. Daddy, you can tell Sol we're ready to go. My date is here now. Oh, and you and Mom better get used to him, because we're in love."

Bennett pulled her close and kissed her. "I totally agree with what you just said."

* * * * *

Dear Reader,

They say Italy is a place for lovers. In my frequent travels across the world, no other place has inspired such desire and truth from me. *From My Heart* is a story that centers on matters of the heart. How many times have we been burdened with regret after the end of a meaningful relationship? How often does one find the courage to let go of the bitterness and explore love again?

On the most romantic day of the year, an encounter between two strangers changes their faith and belief in second chances. Personally, I've never felt that kind of dynamic physical attraction. But in my heart, I know it exists. If you read my stories based on the passion of Italian men you know what you are in store for—undeniable love and proof of second chances.

Sienna Mynx

Acknowledgments

I want to thank my fans (the Mynxers) for continuing this journey with me. Also, I'd like to thank my author friends who continue to nurture and encourage the storyteller in me: Erosa Knowles, Jackie Kelly, Renee Wynn and Pepper Pace. Through the years, I've learned and grown as a writer and a woman because of you. Cheers! Here's to so many more fun, sexy, naughty, good girl/bad boy stories to come.

FROM MY HEART

Sienna Mynx

Chapter 1

"What is this!"

The words leaped off the screen. Any other woman so close to her wedding day would have been angry, frustrated and maybe a bit panicked noticing such a glaring mistake. Not Aniyah. She'd walked on clouds and slid down rainbows with her arms in the air ever since the six-carat diamond ring was slid onto her finger.

"Denton! Come here!"

Leave it to her man to make such a silly mistake. From the day of the proposal to now, Aniyah had taken the lead on everything needed to plan and coordinate the wedding. Denton had been given one job, to spend a few hours while they were on a home vacation this week reviewing the seating arrangement. Who else should decide where his side of family would sit at the reception? Her? Not for a family who frowned at their engagement and whispered that she was just using him to get her struggling acting career off the ground. And typical of Denton, he'd given it half the attention required.

Aniyah shook her head and expelled a deep sigh. She spoke loud enough for him to hear. "So according to you, Buster, Aunt Clara's seeing-eye German shepherd, is married to your aunt Louise. C'mon, Denton! The only reason we have Buster on the invite is because Clara is blind. Remember, you were supposed to put them at a table with family members who wouldn't mind a dog sniffing at their feet while they ate wedding cake." Aniyah dropped her head back in exasperation and closed her eyes. "Did you even try to go through the seating arrangement like I asked?"

She waited. She was certain Denton would run off a list of excuses why this mistake was something she should handle. What her sweet fiancé didn't understand was that they were a team now. Even before she took his name and had the responsibility of being his wife.

Silence spoke for Denton. Aniyah opened her eyes and listened intently for him. She glanced behind her to realize she was alone.

"Oh, good grief," she sighed and pushed back from the breakfast nook, where she had spread out the the reception hall contracts and the little pearl buttons her auntie Donna wanted to make sure she had sewn in on the train of her dress. Auntie Donna had been a mother to her since she was three years old. The pearls were once worn by Aniyah's own mother on her wedding day.

When she stood she must have done so too quickly. A cramp gripped the back of Aniyah's neck and sent a sharp pain down her spine. "Ow." She grimaced. She looked down to the chair and realized she'd been sitting in it for over four hours and hadn't seen or heard from Denton since her work had begun. *Strange.* She stretched and yawned, her vision sweeping the lower level of the loft for him. They'd dated for three long years before he had finally popped the question. Her acting career and his job as a celebrity chef on one of the most popular reality shows kept their schedules in constant conflict. But not anymore. She had one priority—to be Mrs. Denton Jones.

Aniyah looked at the bauble on her finger. She loved to stare at it and often found herself doing so when they made love. Was that strange?

"Denton?" she said softly. He did not answer. If he had decided to leave, he would've had to come her way. He was there, but ignoring her. Why?

Aniyah placed her hands to her hips and stared up the spiral staircase that led to the single bedroom. The sky windows allowed a perfect view of the stars at night but captured all the heat of the Chicago sun during the day. She was glad they'd finally agreed she'd move out of her cramped apartment into his spacious loft instead of buying a house in the suburbs after the wedding.

"Sweetheart? Did you hear me calling you?" she yelled up to the top floor. No answer. Aniyah gave in. She marched up the stairs. She found Denton in his bathroom. He'd remodeled the year before and the bathroom was almost equal in size to the bedroom. The entire room was covered in black granite with silver trim. Very masculine. He'd even gone as far as installing a black marble toilet that had an inside light so you didn't have to turn on the bathroom light at night to find it. They would definitely have to redecorate.

Denton stood before the tall mirror. He glanced at her reflection in the glass. He dismissed her and continued to swipe the straight razor across his jaw. Aniyah knew he was in one of his moods. She let go of her own frustration before she walked in and hugged his waist. He rinsed the shaving cream down the sink. She pressed her cheek against the strong arch of his back and enjoyed the warmth and body heat in her arms. She loved the smell of him after he had freshly showered and shaved.

Denton was six foot two. He had deep brown skin, a dark thick mustache and silky black brows over eyes the color of honey. He was what she and her friends referred to as a metrosexual yummy, all the way down to his manicured nails and tailored business suits. He had more money and fame than any man in the business she'd ever dated. He was the best support system she ever needed financially, emotionally and, of course, physically. She'd fallen in love with him the day he stepped up behind her and offered to pay for her coffee. Tall, impeccably dressed and smelling of spice and sophistication, he had all the qualities necessary to disarm her usual instinct to avoid strangers. He was one stranger she'd love to get dangerous with. That's why she'd patiently waited for this happiness of soon being his wife.

"Did you even take the time to look at the seating chart?" she asked and peppered his back with light kisses. "You put your aunt's dog as your other aunt's husband."

"Aunt who?" he said and bristled.

"Never mind, I fixed it. By the way, you still have to get fitted for your tux. They called and said you missed two appointments."

"I'm filming for the food and wine festival," he said.

"Oh, yeah, I forgot. Well, you have to find time, sweetheart. And the fitting for your brothers is this Sunday—" The words trailed off into his uninterested silence. She let go of his waist and stepped back.

"What's up?" she asked. "You upset about something?"

"You finished?" he answered and rinsed his hands.

"What?"

"Are you finished!" He wiped his face and then tossed the rag into the sink. He then turned on her as if she were some petulant child. His dark brows lowered and his eyes pierced in a way she found familiar.

"What's wrong?" she asked.

"I swear, babe, when you get to talking about the wedding, you can't stop running your mouth," he said.

She masked her hurt with a soft chuckle. But the barb stung. No, his words pierced. She felt it right to the center of her heart. She double blinked at him as he stared down at her.

"All you do is talk about this wedding. Day after day. Nothing else ever comes out of your mouth."

"Why is that a bad thing?" Aniyah asked. "We're getting married in two weeks."

"Why! Why? Because..." He paused. "Oh, hell, this is going to be hard."

Denton pressed his lips together and leaned back on his hands, which gripped the edge of the granite sink. He didn't have to say the words. A woman knows. She knows when her man is happy. A woman in love can sense when her man is hurt or sad. It's in his voice, his body language, his eyes. Aniyah had noticed the way he rolled his eyes when someone brought up the wedding, lately, and how he'd make love to her instead of talking about her dress or the caterers. What had she done wrong to bring them to this point? Love him?

"Tell me. What's the problem?" she asked and cringed at the pathetic, weepy way her voice surrounded the question.

"I was going to talk about this at dinner. But we might as well get into it now," Denton said.

"Get into it?" she repeated.

Denton wiped his hand down his face. He did this when he fought back frustration and weighed her reaction against his confession. She could feel her heart rupturing beneath her breast. Her breathing became labored and her throat incredibly dry. She kept swallowing. One thing was now clear. She hadn't imagined the lack of interest Denton had shown since they began planning the wedding. She'd simply ignored it.

"You know what, get dressed. We can talk about this after you cool off," she said. She turned to leave but Denton caught her wrist. He pulled her back over to him. "I need to call my aunt. Stop—and, and, and…"

"I love you, Aniyah. I do. But this—it's too much, babe, even for me," he said.

"Fine. The festival is huge. You're the top chef. Mega pressure. I get it. I'll deal with the seating arrangement." She gripped the sides of his face and gave him a soft kiss. "You have to get involved here, honey. It's not just my wedding. It's your day too. You have no problem telling me what you like, what makes you unhappy, how is this any different? Let's not stress over it. Here's what you can do…"

"Stop talking," he said.

She did as he asked.

"I don't want to get married," he blurted.

She laughed. "Of course you do."

"Babe, I love you, I do. But marriage? I can't. I really did think I could do this, but I made a mistake. Let's take a break and then maybe we can rethink it, just a short break, a year or…"

Aniyah slapped him. She'd never hit anyone in her life before. Her palm stung. Stunned, full of shameful regret, she shuffled back on her feet and nearly fell flat on her rump. She recovered and backed away from him.

He didn't react. Or maybe he did—how could she really know when she couldn't see his face through her tears?

Aniyah fled into the bedroom and Denton followed. "You asshole! You proposed to *me*. You told my aunt, my friends, you said...you said that you wanted to spend your life with me!"

Aniyah took off in the wrong direction. She meant to head for the stairs. Instead, she stopped at the bed and put her hands to her face. Her misery felt like a steel weight chained to her heart. The proposal and every promise he'd ever made to her now on instant replay in her mind. She had heard and seen him give the performance of his life, clearly. *Bravo!* Denton Jones wanted *her* to be his wife. He'd said so. Now she had to believe he and his fake promises were all a lie.

"You pressured me," he said.

She spun on him. Rage swelled in her like a nuclear cloud. She felt her cheeks and chest puff with indignation. Her nails cut into her palms from her hands being clenched into tight fists. "Pressure? I pressured you? I spent three years of my life making sure there was no pressure, you jerk!"

Denton put his hands to his shaved head. "That's not what I mean, sweetheart."

"What do you mean?" she shouted. "Say it! Say it!"

"There are different kinds of pressure. Okay! You kept talking about getting married like it was the natural step for us. It isn't. I love you, I do, but I don't want to be married to anyone. I thought I could do this because frankly, we're hot together. Everyone sees it. And hell, call me a bastard, but I don't want to give you up to another man. But I can't get married! Not to you. Not to any woman. I need to be my own man."

The truth was the final blow. Aniyah refused to spend

another minute taking in his nonsense. She ran for the stairs, but Denton stopped her. He tried to embrace her. The jerk even had the nerve to try to kiss her! She fought back. Who needed this crap from a man who was supposed to be her hero? Who needed Denton Jones? But the truth was she did. And that was what hurt the most. She had put all her dreams and faith into *them* and not herself. She'd been a fool. She shoved her way out of his arms and went down the stairs in tears.

"Where are you going?" Denton shouted after her. "Don't leave. Please, babe, let me explain."

Wounded with humiliation, she grabbed her purse and her car keys. When she tried to run for the door he had already reached it, blocking her only exit. She was forced to look up into his lying face, and the tears flowed.

"You want space. Fine. You're free, Denton. No pressure. I don't ever want to see you again."

"That's ridiculous! Save the hysteria for your acting classes," he shouted. "This is why it can never work between us. I want a girlfriend, not a wife. That doesn't mean I don't love you."

"No. It means you don't know me. I'm not settling for anyone who can't commit to me. Three years and now you don't know what you want? Get out of my way!" she said.

With no other choice left, Denton finally stepped aside. Aniyah paused. "Mama," she said softly.

She glanced back to her mother's pearls—she'd left them on the breakfast nook. She walked over and swept them all into a nearby small plastic baggie with extreme care. She didn't bother with the wedding planning book or even the laptop he had bought her for Christmas. She had her mother's pearls and that was enough. She wiped her tears and straightened her back. She walked out on the promise they'd made to each other and the man she'd been prepared to love for the rest of her life. And it hurt. What hurt more was the way he closed the door on her. She glanced back once over her shoulder and saw the look on his face. It didn't mirror the pain she carried in her heart. It was a look of relief.

Chapter 2

"Aniyah? Sweetheart, are you in here?" Samantha called out to her.

The door to her bedroom opened. Aniyah looked up from her tearstained pillow and tried to speak. Her voice was gone. So much crying and screaming through the night had exhausted her both mentally and physically.

"Sweetheart. I drove through the night. Oh, honey, stop crying, I promise you will be okay." Samantha walked over to the bed. Aniyah reached for her best friend and wept in her arms. She cried the last of her tears. At least for the night.

"I'm sorry you had to leave your retreat. I'm so sorry," Aniyah said.

"Don't be sorry. I was sick of those meditating robots. I'm just glad I broke the rules and checked my messages. Did you turn your phone off after? I've been calling."

Aniyah nodded that she had before she dropped back

in exhaustion on her pillow. Her bed was covered in crumpled tissues. Her face was swollen from her grief.

"Okay, start from the beginning." Samantha tossed her purse aside. She sat on the bed as a doctor would for any despondent patient. But there was nothing Samantha could do to fix this. There was nothing anyone could do.

"I told you already. He called off the wedding, Sam."

"You had a fight. That happens. He has the wedding jitters or something," Samantha reasoned.

"No. No. No! This wasn't just a fight. He wanted out. He acted like I had forced him to propose. I feel so stupid. Three years with that asshole and he all but accused me of dragging him to the altar. I feel like someone died. It hurts in my stomach, my head, my heart." She clutched her chest.

"Hush now," Samantha said. She looked down to Aniyah's lap. "What is this?"

Aniyah wiped her tears. She couldn't speak. Her thoughts were clogged with emotion.

"Oh, my, this is beautiful. Did you do this?"

The gold necklace had four pearls on it. When she got home she'd spent the first six hours working on it. Being busy helped. It wasn't the best work she'd done, but it was nice enough to preserve her mother's pearls. "They were supposed to be on my wedding dress."

The tears came once more. Samantha knocked away the snot tissues and eased into bed next to her. She lay on her side and looked down at Aniyah. "It's okay. I promise we will figure it out."

"I thought he loved me. I thought he was the one. He's right. I've been the one pushing. For everything. What is wrong with me?"

"It's not a bad thing to fall in love. It just a hard thing

to stay in love. A man has to want it in his life. If he doesn't, then it's best you find out now. Right?"

"I guess," she sniffed. "I put everything into this relationship. What am I going to do now?"

Aniyah had dumped her entire savings into the wedding. The best acting jobs she gotten were through Denton's contacts. After the proposal she switched gears and taken some voice-over classes. But that wasn't a lucrative business for her.

"What do you want to do? Talk to him? Call your aunt? Call your agent? What?" Samantha asked.

"No. It's over. And you know my agent is his agent. He won't do anything for me. Probably will drop me before the end of the week." Aniyah wept. "Do me a favor."

"Anything, sweetheart."

"I'll need you to make some calls for me. Please. I can't deal with anyone right now. Just…tell people…it's over. The wedding is off."

"Okay, I'll do that." Samantha smiled. "We'll figure it out."

Aniyah passed a mirror. That was her first mistake. The woman reflected back to her was gaunt with bloodshot eyes. Her hair was tangled in knots that seemed to reach all the way to the roots. Her lips were chapped, and her eyes were swollen and puffy around the lids. She was stunned at the ashy, dull luster to her medium-brown complexion. She imagined that this must be what a corpse looked like after being abandoned to rot. Nearly two weeks ago her heart had been broken. Not enough time to properly heal.

Aniyah picked up her cell phone and turned it on. That was her second mistake. After the breakup she'd gone radio silent. She wouldn't even turn on the television.

She just sat in bed and read her favorite books over and over while binge eating corn chips and mint ice cream. Samantha gave up three days in and let her mope, but then Samantha got an acting gig that called for her to return to Atlanta.

Aniyah was alone.

The phone vibrated in Aniyah's hand. She had thirty-two new voice mail messages. She sat at her kitchen table and felt the tears welling in her eyes. When she looked at all the messages from caterers, reception halls, friends and family she expected to see a call from Denton. He should be begging for forgiveness by now. But there wasn't one missed call from her ex-fiancé. There were no messages. He had truly abandoned her.

Did everyone know? Was this what it was like to be left at the altar? The humiliation was debilitating.

The phone rang in her hands. Startled, Aniyah looked down at an international number she didn't know.

"Ah, hello?" she answered.

"*Buon giorno!* Am I speaking to Signora Jones?"

Aniyah wasn't sure how to respond. The person assumed she was married. Aniyah glanced up to the wall calendar to realize that yesterday would have actually been her wedding, February 11. In all her depression she had lost track of time. She had even managed to block out the day she was supposed to be married.

"Hello? Hello, signora? Are you there?"

"I—ah—I am. Who is this?"

"My name is Gabriella, but most here call me Zia. When you arrive you are welcome to as well. I am calling to confirm your arrival to Camogli. We are excited for you and your new husband. The festival has already begun, but you will arrive in time for San Valentino! We have so much planned. What time will your flight land in Genoa? We will have driver sent for you."

"Flight...yeah, uh, I think I land at noon?" Aniyah said.

"*Va bene!* We welcome your arrival. We welcome you. Ciao for now!"

"Ciao." Aniyah smiled. She had forgotten about the honeymoon. It was the only thing that Denton had paid for. She insisted on paying for her wedding, though he had offered. She wanted to prove her independence. Sure it took her forever to save for the expense, and right now every spare dime she had was spent. But it was *her* big day. She was determined to start their life out as partners no matter how much more money he made than her. They had planned to go to the most romantic place in the world: a small village called Camogli in Liguria, Italy, that held a big lovers' event on St. Valentine's Day. The private seafront resort, Mi Amore, catered to no more than twenty guests and was open to married couples only. And it would be the perfect getaway.

Aniyah got up and found her old laptop. She opened it and crossed her fingers that it still worked. After ten minutes of trying, it connected to her email and she accessed the account. After a few searches she pulled up the itinerary. Her flight left in six hours. She called the airline to confirm her ticket was there. It was. Denton hadn't canceled it.

What should she do? Should she go? How could she go? Denton made considerably more money than she did and had paid for the first-class airline tickets and the expense of the resort in advance. She, however, wanted to do her part. The sad truth was she was broke. She and her aunt had spent lavishly on the wedding, and all of her refundable deposits were being held up. There was no time to negotiate the funds for a trip to Italy. No money. To her horror, the laptop blinked to a black screen, then a blue screen.

"Shoot! Shoot! Shoot!"

She desperately tried turning it off and back on, but each time she got the blue screen. It was broken.

Aniyah used the banking app on her phone to look up her checking and savings account. What she discovered was pitiful, but it might work, if she were frugal.

In her room, Aniyah dragged out her suitcase and makeup bag. She grabbed every stylish sundress she could find in her closet. She didn't realize it then, but later she would remember that she was smiling.

"So let me get this straight. You are on your way to the airport. You're still going to Italy?" her aunt Donna asked.

"Yep! Traffic is crazy today. If I don't get there in the next twenty minutes, there is no way I can make this flight." Aniyah slammed her hand on the steering wheel when a car cut her off.

"Slow down. You haven't called me in over a week. Your cousin and I were on our way to come see you. The wedding planners, the church, you haven't returned any of their calls. I spoke to Samantha. She had to contact all your guests and tell them the wedding is off. And you lost most of your deposits, honey. Do you even have any money?"

"Auntie…"

"Don't auntie me! You're being reckless again. Impulsive! Leaving the country? You haven't healed. And you need to deal with Denton. That is the responsible thing to do."

"What I need is to get away from Chicago. From him. And don't worry, Denton could care less."

"What about money? You still haven't answered me. I know you don't have much. You emptied your accounts for that wedding. I got your creditors calling here. And you haven't had an acting job in months."

Aniyah sighed. Her aunt was an expert in all the things she hadn't done or didn't have. She was really killing her mood. "I will be gone for seven days. I have enough money. The resort is all paid for, including meals. I have enough to get me through it. Don't worry, Auntie. I just… I need to do this for me."

"Let me put some money in your account," her aunt said.

"No!" Aniyah said. "You have done enough. I'm tired of having to call you to fix my problems. I even had Denton fixing my problems. The wedding is off and I'm okay. I'll go to Italy, soak up some sun and clear my head."

"Call me when you land. Promise me!" her aunt said.

"I promise! Love you. Ciao!"

Aniyah drove up into the park-and-pay at the airport. It would be nine dollars a day. She chewed on her bottom lip. She had lied to her aunt. She had about three hundred dollars to her name. She would have to set aside sixty-three dollars for her return. That made a dent in her limited funds. Seven days in Italy with $240? What did that translate to in euros? Could she really pull this off? She parked. It would be so easy to call her aunt and ask her for another loan. It would be even more responsible to stay home and deal with the financial fallout of her canceled wedding. However, Aniyah never liked life when it was easy or responsible. She wanted adventure. She wanted Italy.

Chapter 3

Niccolo Montenegro walked the line of his employees. His tanned olive-brown skin and well-groomed appearance was a stark contrast to the grief-stricken man who had left them a year ago. Niccolo had changed and he was determined to let them all know it.

His hands were clasped behind his back. His seafront hotel had once been the most popular along the Italian Riviera and had catered to the affluent. But a year and half after he left its care to his aunt and cousin, the fortune his family had acquired over fifty years had nearly been depleted. He'd had to return. This was supposed to be the salvation of his dead wife's dream while he was away tending to his bitterness over his loss. He was a fool to have turned his company over to them. He was a coward for leaving. And with only three days left before the festival. He was desperate to find a way to save them all. If something didn't change for all of them quickly, he'd have to close the doors.

"I trusted you. And look at this place. Look at it! *Patetico!*" he said. He picked up a paper heart sprinkled in confetti from the reception desk. He tossed it to the floor and dusted his hands. "I'm back now. No more freebies, no more handouts. We have three days left until the festival, and we will turn a profit this year."

The employees exchanged looks, and only a few nodded in agreement. Niccolo had seen the books. The place was at half capacity. They were in the red. Nothing short of a miracle from Saint Valentino himself could save them. After Mya died two years ago he'd tried to keep their dream alive. Grief, however, was like an anvil hung from his neck. Even the smallest attempt to move away from the pain required so much physical and emotional strength he collapsed over and over under the weight of it. And this place, with all its beauty, celebrations of love and happiness, had strangled the life out of him. He'd had no choice but to run away. The isolation made the empty grief and despair harden his heart, yet he'd healed. If it weren't for his aunt calling and explaining the state of their affairs, he might never have returned.

"Niccolo," Zia Gabriella said.

"I'm not done!" he silenced her. "All-inclusive? Zia? You and Elaina made Mi Amore all-inclusive? *Dannazione!* If you are going to take away every opportunity to turn a profit, then the cost to stay here must compensate! And what have you done to bring in more couples? Several hotels have all kinds of parties and festivities? You decorate with a few hearts and glitter and offer free alcohol? That's it!"

The assistant manager and event coordinator of the Mi Amore was Elaina, his third cousin. And she was nine months pregnant. She stood at the center of the employee gathering with her eyes lowered in shame and her hands resting on her belly. Yelling at his elderly aunt and pregnant cousin made him feel like an ass. He had all but turned the business over to them after Mya's death. He could not believe the dire financial state they faced in just a year.

Elaina's gaze lifted, and he could see tears on her cheeks. Full of exasperation, Niccolo threw his hands up in defeat and stormed away. He was only a step into his office when his aunt Gabriella charged in after him. She slammed the door behind her.

"Basta!" his aunt shouted. "Niccolo, how dare you treat them that way? Elaina? Have you lost all of your senses?"

"Has she? We are in debt because—"

"Because of you!" His aunt pointed a finger at him. "You left us. You disappeared when we were all grieving the death of Mya. We did the best we could to keep this place from sinking into debt, but we've missed her, too. Now you return and it is our fault you're so unhappy?"

"None of this is about my happiness," he countered. "This is a business, Zia!"

"None of this is about the business. It's about your grief. I see it in you, Niccolo. Sure, you look fancy in that suit and with that tan, but I see it in you! If you can't let your misery go, then you should leave. I'd rather see Mi Amore close its doors than become bitterly unsavable like you!"

The words hit him hard. Before he could counter, she stormed out of the office. Niccolo sat on his desk. He sucked in a deep breath to calm his temper. Mya was good at teaching him balance. She'd been the one that grounded him. He'd become a better man because of her. Now who would he be without her?

Images of her and their life together became the focus of his memory. He saw her rushing through the office looking for some forgotten token she wanted to bestow on a guest. He'd have to pull her from a task by both arms to steal a kiss.

The price of recalling the sweetness of his wife's lips beneath his own was another punch to his gut, along with the memory of watching her die in his arms. Niccolo put his face in his hands.

Someone screamed.

Niccolo stood. It was a woman's scream. And it was followed by another and then another...

The driver spoke little English, but during the drive along the coastal highways out of Genoa to Liguria he made sure to point out some of the most beautiful scenery. Aniyah soaked in everything, from the sun to the architecture of buildings and gardens that had to be centuries old. And to her delight, Camogli was near the sea, where the water sparkled a deep turquoise blue. She used her cell phone to record some of it and snapped a few pictures of the yellow, pink and blue flowers blooming on the sides of the road. And then they traveled along a narrow one-way street between tall buildings and up steep inclines. She could see into the stores. A few local people even smiled at her. Aniyah smiled in return.

"We are here," the driver said.

She leaned forward and looked out to a gated villa covered in wild vines and decorated with red, white and green ribbons.

"Oh, wow! Is this it?" she asked.

"Si, signora, benvenuto in Camogli!" The driver wel-

comed her to Camogli before he got of the little box-shaped cab and walked on his short thick legs to the gate. He pulled one open and then another before returning. They drove up to the tall wooden abbey doors. Aniyah didn't bother to wait for him to open her door. She was quickly out the car, soaking in every detail.

"It's beautiful. I can't believe how serene this place is," she said. "How old is it?"

"I think, aye, it's old. Eh? Two hundred? Yes, two hundred years."

"Wow?" she gasped.

"Salvatore Montenegro built it with his brothers."

"That's so cool." Aniyah snapped a few more pics and then sent them to her aunt to make sure Donna knew she would be okay.

The driver walked over to the back of the car and removed her luggage.

"Even the air tastes sweet." Aniyah chuckled. She turned her face up toward the sun and inhaled deeply with her eyes closed. She spun around in a circle with her arms extended. Two weeks of tears and misery, a ten-hour flight to paradise, and she felt renewed. Then another cold gust of wind hit her and she covered her arms. It dawned on her that she never checked the weather. She just assumed she was going to the tropics. Those passing her were covered in jackets and long pants. It was February and freezing in Chicago. But in typical Aniyah style she left every coat she owned at home. She shook her head and smiled.

When she stopped she locked eyes with a couple who had stopped to stare at her. The young blonde woman smiled and her tall companion winked. Aniyah nodded to the couple. They walked off hand in hand behind a troupe following a person who looked to be their guide.

"Guests?" she asked the driver.

He dragged her luggage over to her.

"*Si*, signora, you are in the Golfo Paradiso, a lover's paradise," he said.

The resort was exclusive to couples only. It was one of the reasons she'd chosen this one over the less expensive ones. The people expected to pick up newlyweds. The lies she told had started at the airport when the driver had asked about her husband. It dawned on her that the deception would have to continue for the duration of the stay. She'd have to keep to herself and not draw any attention to her circumstances.

"*Andiamo,*" the driver huffed. He lifted both suitcases and waddled toward the abbey doors.

Aniyah was quick to follow. She glanced back once more at the couples leaving for their tour. It would be Valentine's Day soon. God help her.

When she entered the resort, a woman screamed. It scared the hell out of her. The few people gathered in the front of the establishment all froze. A young woman with long raven hair, doubled over holding a very swollen pregnant belly. An older woman shouted the name Niccolo while two younger men half carried, half dragged the pregnant woman to the sofa. Aniyah's driver dropped her luggage and went after them to offer help.

"Niccolo!" another person shouted, and the woman continued to scream through her tears.

A man appeared. Her gaze froze on his broad shoulders and beautifully proportioned masculine form as he walked over to those shouting and pacing around the pregnant woman. He was tall, dressed in dark slacks and a hunter green shirt that had sleeves rolled up to the bend of his elbows. She didn't see his face, but his presence calmed everyone. The man knelt next to the

woman, who was now panting as if she were about to
deliver. He whispered something in her ear as he rubbed
her belly with care. The woman smiled and appeared to
relax, just a little.

"Scusimi, signora!" A woman grabbed her arm.

"Ah? Yes?" Aniyah answered.

"Are you a *dottore*? Are you?" the woman asked.

"Me? No. I, uh, went to nursing school for six weeks
but dropped out because…"

"Nurse! Aye! *Infermiera! Infermiera!*"

"Wait, what? What are you saying? No, no, no, *infermiera…*" Aniyah protested.

The woman dragged her over to the small gathering
of people.

"Niccolo, she's a nurse," the woman said in Italian,
which Aniyah couldn't understand.

He glanced up at her. His ruggedly handsome face was
vaguely familiar. She'd met many actors and models in
her line of work. All of them had certain characteristics
a director looked for, a look that would capture a girl's
interest in a print ad or a thirty-second commercial. This
man had that look. His face was bronzed by many days
in the wind and sun. He had thick, curly jet-black hair
cut short with long sideburns. And his eyes were dark
brown swirls of beauty ringed in long dark lashes. His
lips were perfect in symmetry under a thin mustache that
connected to a trimmed goatee. And he was probably the
same age as Denton, in his early thirties.

The moment their eyes met, she felt her heart flutter.
If they were in a scene, the director would've yelled "cut"
over her stupefied staring. *Jeesh, do they make all the
men in Italy this way?* And then he spoke with a deeper
accent than the woman holding her arm so tight it felt
like she had pincers instead of hands.

* * *

The woman before Niccolo stopped his heart. He had to blink twice to clear his vision. For a moment, a brief one, he thought his beloved had returned to him from the dead. He nearly spoke her name: *Mya*.

But the petite black woman before him in fancy red shoes and a white sundress had thick curly hair, and wore bright red lipstick, which Mya never did. Still, she was his dead wife in every other way. Her slender waist, fine hips and shapely thighs with toned legs were nothing compared to the perfect bosom he looked past to connect with her dark brown eyes.

"Are you a nurse?" he heard himself ask in Italian. He repeated the question in English. Because he knew she was not from his world. Just as Mya had not been.

Her glossy, plump red lips parted and her white teeth sparkled beneath. She glanced to his cousin Elaina, and when she looked at him once more a surge of curious desire stirred in his gut. What if she spoke and her voice was like Mya's? What then? Was this some kind of cosmic joke? Could reincarnation happen in a matter of two years? No, it was crazy to think it. But damn it, something was going on. Where had she come from?

Elaina screamed again. He snapped out of his own stupor and returned his attention to his sweet cousin. She was suffering. He stroked her round tummy and whispered in her ear.

"Forgive me, Elaina. I am so sorry for arguing. Don't worry. We will protect the baby." He leaned in and kissed Elaina's tearstained cheek.

"The medics are coming for her. But the festival may delay them. What should we do, Niccolo?" Margareta asked.

He swept his cousin up in his arms. *"Andiamo!"*

* * *

One look into his eyes and she was rendered deaf, dumb and mute. The only other man that had that effect on her was Denton. And this man was nothing like her ex-fiancé.

The older woman grabbed her hand and pulled her along. Aniyah could do nothing but follow. So this was Niccolo. He carried the weeping pregnant woman in his arms as a savior would. He was strong. He walked with his back erect, his stride long and confident. The man with the dreamy eyes and sexy name would help the pregnant woman, she was certain. But what the hell was she doing being dragged into the rescue?

He placed the woman down on a bed. The room was quaint. It had a bed and dresser and French doors that led to a balcony. The cool-colored walls and the lazy swipes of the ceiling fan gave a soothing calmness that everyone needed.

An older woman removed the weeping woman's panties while others put pillows behind her back. Niccolo gave instructions in his native language to the people entering and leaving the room, bringing in the things that he needed.

"Qual è il tuo nome?" he asked. Aniyah shrugged her shoulders to indicate she didn't understand him.

"Your name, signora?" Niccolo asked. "What is your name?"

"Ah, I'm, um, Aniyah," she stammered.

"I'm going to need your help, Aniyah. Wash your hands, *per favore.*"

"I'm not a nurse," she said.

"You are now," he assured her. "I'll do the work. You keep my family back so I can get the baby."

"Your family? Are all of them your family?" Aniyah counted at least thirteen additional people in the room.

Niccolo chuckled. "Most of them, yes."

"Are you a doctor?" she asked.

He gave a half smile. "I am now."

"But shouldn't we take her to a hospital, get a real doctor?"

"The nearest *ospedale* is thirty-two kilometers away. She won't make it. Please, *signora*, help Niccolo," said the older woman in the room.

It suddenly dawned on Aniyah that they were going to deliver the baby there. No way in hell was she ready for that. It was one of the main reasons she'd dropped out of nursing school. The sight of blood made her faint. She turned to leave when another woman rushed in with more towels. They were all speaking Italian. No. They were shouting in Italian. Their collective voices were so loud she could barely hear Niccolo's direction. She couldn't understand anyone.

"Hurry! I need your help!" Niccolo said again.

Aniyah hadn't washed her hands. There was so much pushing to get into the room that she knew she couldn't escape. Feeling a bit light-headed, she went to Niccolo as if in a trance. A woman stopped her and wiped her hands with a warm soapy rag. She was then pushed to her knees next to Niccolo.

"Hold the pillow. We don't want the baby to come out and slip to the floor," he said. This meant she had to play catcher with Niccolo. The pregnant woman had been pulled down to the edge of the bed. She was now holding her knees. Her legs were parted. She was crying and screaming in pain while one woman dabbed her sweaty forehead and another woman on the bed behind her rubbed her back. Several others were in the room praying, which sounded like chanting. Each had a rosary in her hands. Every single minute that lapsed felt surreal.

"Are you ready? Aniyah? The baby is coming," Niccolo said with a deep chuckle.

"I think I'm going to throw up," Aniyah answered. She looked down. *She never should have looked down!* The head of the baby was crowning. Niccolo was yelling something in Italian. The others were now saying the same things. She guessed they were all telling Elaina to push.

Blood and a baby came out. The room spun and darkened. Aniyah collapsed.

Chapter 4

"*Stai bene?*" a man asked.

His voice was so soothing she wanted to emerge from the darkness. Her eyes fluttered and opened. She saw several faces and had to blink repeatedly for her vision to clear. Then one face became her sole focus. It was Niccolo. He wiped her forehead with sincere concern denting his brow. He glanced up to the older woman who was on the other side of her and nodded.

"She'll be okay," he said.

"What happened?" Aniyah asked and tried to sit up. The minute she did, her head ached as if she had suffered trauma to the back of it. "Ow!"

"Careful, *cara*," he said softly. He sat her upright and made sure she was comfortable. "You hit your head pretty hard when you fainted."

"I fainted!" Aniyah said and touched the lump at the back of her head underneath her curls. "Oh, my God, I'm so embarrassed."

The old woman nodded. *"Si*, signora. You fainted."

A baby cried. Aniyah looked to the bed. Elaina was holding her tiny infant, soothing her. She glanced to Aniyah and smiled. *"Grazie,"* Elaina said.

The others were cleaning up. Aniyah could see traces of blood on the sheets and wet towels. She closed her eyes and felt the urge to puke rise in her throat. "I have to get out of here."

"Come," Niccolo said. Before she could object, he eased his arm around her waist and helped her stand. She put her arm around his shoulder. It felt natural but inappropriate, since she liked the comfort. He helped her to the door. They walked out of the room and the strength returned to Aniyah's legs.

"I'm okay. Thank you," she said and pulled away from him.

"I am sorry you were dragged into this drama. We looked for your husband to tell him where you were."

"Uh, he's not here," she said as she rubbed the soreness from the back of her head. When she looked into his eyes, she saw the concern. "Work. It was last-minute, so I, uh, came alone," Aniyah said.

"But you're newly married," Niccolo said.

"Yeah, well, my husband has different priorities. Can I just go to my room, please?" Aniyah asked. Niccolo looked at her for a moment as if she'd cursed him. Maybe her tone had been a bit sharp. However, the embarrassment over lying to a stranger made her feel defensive.

"Of course. I've had everything brought upstairs to your room. We've upgraded your suite." He gave her a thin-lipped smile, dug into his pocket and drew out an old-fashioned key. On the ring was the room number. "Thank you for your help. Enjoy your stay."

"Wait. I didn't mean to be so rude."

He walked off without a second glance.

"Damn it, Aniyah!" She stamped her foot. She looked down at the key in her hand and then back down the hall. When he'd said everything had been taken to her room, did he mean her purse and phone, too? She had nothing. Aniyah walked back to the front of the resort. The paramedics had arrived. They were being directed to the room where the young woman and her child bonded.

"Signora, hello," a voice said from behind her. She turned and saw her approaching fast. It was the kind older woman who had asked if she was a nurse when she'd arrived. "I'm Gabriella, but they call me Zia. I called you to confirm your reservation. Remember?"

"Yes. Yes! Hi, I just need to get to my room. I don't have my purse or cell phone. And I'm not sure where room 223 is."

Gabriella smiled. "We have everything ready for you, Mrs. Jones. Come let me show you."

Aniyah followed Gabriella back through the resort to a side stairwell, and then up a flight of stairs. The halls were narrow, but she passed at least six rooms on the way to another stairwell that was much more cramped and narrow. They climbed the stairs to a private wing.

"This is our honeymoon suite. Totally private. My nephew Niccolo is on the other end of the hall. No worries. He won't disturb you," she said.

"The woman who had the baby, what was her name?"

"Elaina."

"Are Elaina and the baby going to be all right?" Aniyah asked.

"Oh, yes. I know it frightened you. We are so sorry you were caught up in the confusion. It's a very exciting time for the family. A new baby. Ah, here we are," Gabriella said. She used the key Aniyah gave her and opened the door. "This is a very nice room. Please. Have a look."

Aniyah stepped inside and her gaze swept the room. It was quite spacious. The floors were yellow, orange and brown mosaic tile. Most of the furnishings, including two dressers, a vanity desk and a chaise, were modest, and she understood why—the most charming and exquisite piece of furniture was the king-size canopy bed. It had sheer draping that was far more romantic than she would like. The bed was made for lovers. Across the bed, the resort staff had sprinkled petals from the beautiful flowers she'd seen blooming all around the villa. And they'd lit several fragrant candles. The windows were open, allowing in a sweet breeze with a hint of the sea. From her room she could see the blue waters of the Golfo Paradiso.

"This is too much," she mumbled.

"It's fine. Tomorrow we celebrate *Innamorati a Camogli,*" Gabriella said. "All day. We have so much planned."

"What does that mean? *Innamorati a Camogli?*" Aniyah asked.

"It means Lovers in Camogli. It takes place every year in the days leading up to St. Valentine's Day. You had to have known about it, to come here with your husband."

"He selected this place for us. Prepaid for it," Aniyah said. The pain in her heart for Denton had numbed. Even her anger had subsided. She was more curious about her future and the beautiful town than interested in dwelling on what they'd shared.

"*Va bene.* Come downstairs and join us around six for dinner. You will love it. And I hope your husband will arrive soon."

"Thank you, Gabriella," she said.

"Call me Zia. *Prego.*"

Aniyah watched her go. She then went to the window

and stared out at the sea. She looked down to the promenade. People were hanging up papier-mâché lanterns, red hearts and ribbons from every light post and building awning. Several men were working off to the east to set up what looked to be a stage. She stepped back and again cursed her choice. You can't heal your heart in the most romantic place in the world. What was she thinking?

Niccolo closed the accounting ledger. They'd wasted four days, doing little to nothing to draw in more people or turn a profit. Prime time for the hotel to profit on the season was the week prior to the festival. Parties and excursions were key for lovers. Tourism was up. Money was being poured into the village to renovate and expand on business interests. So why had Mi Amore fallen so far behind? He almost pushed back from the desk to leave the office but paused. A flyer caught his eye. He pulled it out from under the papers and folders scattered everywhere across the desk. Camogli was having a contest for the local businesses. Many cash prizes. But the one offered for the resort that threw the most lavish and lovingly authentic bash on Valentine's Day would be rewarded a hundred and fifty thousand euros. He couldn't believe it. The money would be enough to renovate and pay down some of their debt. The judging was only two days away.

Niccolo charged out of his office. He went straight to the gardens in search of his aunt. There were several family members who worked for him setting up for dinner. But there was no sign of his aunt. He checked his watch. She had to be in the kitchen. He turned to leave when his gaze lifted to the second-story window. He paused. Aniyah stood there staring out toward the sea. Her smooth brown skin glowed with copper overtones.

Her thick curly dark hair was blown clear from her face. And in the afternoon rays he could see even more of her pretty face. She had a look of loving to pamper herself. She probably didn't have a care in the world. Most beautiful women didn't, he supposed. Her husband was a fool to send her off on a honeymoon alone. What man would?

She never glanced his way. He was grateful. If she had caught the way he stared up at her, she would be offended. What married woman would want another man's desire?

"She reminds you of her, doesn't she?"

Niccolo glanced back at his zia. She stood there staring up at the window where Aniyah had been.

"I know she does. She reminds me of her, too. The moment I saw her I thought of Mya," Zia said.

"I want to talk to you. Why haven't you told me about this?" Niccolo put the flyer in Gabriella's face.

His aunt looked at the paper and then at him with disinterest. "The entire village is competing for that money. We don't have the money or the staff to win."

"So you give up without even trying? This is why we will lose this place. Giving up!" he said.

"Who gave up first, Niccolo? Answer that question," she countered.

"I'm going to the solicitor's office before it closes and entering us in the competition. I'm not giving up."

Zia stepped in his path. "We are family. We can heal together. If you give us a chance. I know delivering Elaina's baby was hard—it had to remind you of—"

"Stop!" Niccolo demanded. "I don't need nurturing, or protecting. What I need is to win the *Innamorati a Camogli*. Can you help me do that?"

His aunt nodded.

"Good. Then focus there," he said and left her standing there with tears in her eyes. He walked out of the garden, heading for town. He'd travel on foot. He needed to clear his head. Mya never got the chance to become a mother. She never got the chance to have any of the things he had promised for them. And that was his fault. He understood now how he could finally let his sweet wife go. He'd save Mi Amore, and the family. He'd do it alone if he had to.

Aniyah couldn't stand it. Ten minutes into dinner and she found an excuse to bring her plate and drink upstairs. All the giggling couples gave her a headache. And the language barrier with those on the staff who took pity on a woman alone was uncomfortable. Now she sat on her bed staring at an Italian television program. She could understand a few of the scenes playing before her, but after several minutes she became bored. Maybe it was best to take a walk. Her own little private walk into town.

She found the Italian translation book she'd bought at the airport and put it in her purse. She eased her feet into comfortable thong sandals and slipped out of the resort without a questioning look from anyone. Lucky for her she had a thin sweater to wear. It was after seven and the temperature had dropped. But a little chill in Italy was nothing compared to the hard winters in Chicago. She could handle it. Every shopkeeper's door was flung open. She stopped at a few and fawned over handmade jewelry, pottery, quilts, puppets, decorative plates and handbags. She was surprised at the few people who were eager to speak English to her. She tried to speak Italian with the aid of her book as best as she could.

Time slipped away from her. Soon she found herself strolling along the seafront promenade. On her right were three story buildings. Each connected to the next with many windows in a range of colors from yellow and orange to melon and pink. To her left was the pier and boats docked and of course the beaches that led out to the sea. A sweet breeze washed over her. She reached into her straw bag and drew out her shawl. She wasn't cold, though it was cool. It felt more like a cleansing. She could feel the small particles of water in the air. She wrapped the shawl around her shoulders and stopped to see a young boy playing his banjo and singing for a small gathering.

The meeting with the village solicitor went well. Niccolo had oversold the resort's ability to compete. Now he was left with twenty-four hours to plan an event that would normally take months to organize. He scratched his head as he thought about how he could pull it off. The singing voice of Pepe drew his attention. The eight-year-old was a distant cousin of his and often came down to the promenade to make money from the tourists. He started toward him to tell him to get home. It was getting late.

When he arrived at the crowd, the first person he saw was Aniyah. She looked up at him and smiled. Niccolo smiled in return. And to his surprise she approached him.

"Hi!"

"Ciao," he said.

"He's pretty good," she said.

"His name is Pepe. He can play the piano, too."

"You know him?" she asked.

"He's my cousin."

"Wow. Is everyone in this town related to you?" She chuckled.

He smiled. "Not everyone."

Pepe finished his song and several people dropped coins in tin cup. He put down his banjo and came over and hugged Niccolo. "You're home, Niccolo. You're home," said Pepe. Niccolo knelt and embraced the boy.

It had been over a year since he'd seen him. He'd grown. He paid attention as Pepe tried to tell him everything that had happened to him in the past year. Niccolo was patient as he listened to his little cousin's tales. All the while he kept glancing to Aniyah. She didn't walk away. She stood there smiling at them both and rubbing her arms to keep warm. When Pepe stopped to catch his breath, Niccolo made the introduction.

"This is Aniyah," he told his cousin. "She's a guest at the hotel."

Aniyah fumbled in her purse. She took out a dollar bill and gave it his cousin. Pepe grabbed her hand and kissed it. Niccolo chuckled.

"I think you've done enough today. Pack up and go home. I will come visit you tomorrow."

"You promise, Niccolo? You will come?"

"I promise," he said and kissed his brow. Pepe waved goodbye to them both and took off down the promenade on his bike.

"He's a talented kid. Can you sing?" she asked.

"I often try. Haven't made as much money as Pepe at it."

She grinned. "Niccolo. About earlier today. I was rude."

"No. No need to apologize. You were probably still in shock," he said.

"Let me make it up to you. A gelato, maybe?" she asked.

"Only if you let me treat," Niccolo said.

"No! It's my apology," she reasoned.

"And I want to be gracious in accepting. Come, I know the store owner."

"Wait? Are you related to him, too?" she asked.

He winked. Aniyah laughed. She walked over with

him to order a chocolate scoop and he got pistachio. They started back down the promenade together. At first he didn't speak. He didn't have to. There were plenty of street vendors to draw her attention. But his curiosity got the best of him.

"Aniyah, where is your jacket?" he asked her.

"Oh? I didn't think about the weather. I thought Italy was sunny all year."

"We are pretty warm, but we enjoy winter too." He shrugged off his jacket.

"No. No. I couldn't. I'm fine. I have my sweater on."

"You're my guest. It would be impolite to let you freeze to death the first day of your visit."

She chuckled. She eased her arms in through the sleeves. *"Grazie,"* she said.

He gave her a curt nod and they continued on their walk.

"Does your husband arrive soon?"

She licked her gelato and didn't answer. He thought to ask her again and then decided not to. Instead he looked up at the moon. It was full. An omen. Maybe even a good sign for what he faced in the next forty-eight hours.

"Are you married?" she asked.

"I'm a widower," he said.

"Oh, I'm sorry. How did she die?"

Niccolo decided not to answer her question. If she didn't want to talk about her husband, he felt no need to discuss his wife. To his relief, she didn't push.

They finished their gelato by the time they reached the end of the promenade. They had walked quite a bit and had said so little. She didn't feel like a stranger to him. She had a calming nature. One that made it easy to be around her without questions.

"Would you like a ride back to the hotel?" he asked.

"A cab?" She frowned and looked around at the people crowding the street. There wasn't a car in sight.

"Not quite. Come with me," he said. She followed.

They walked up a narrow street. Through two very close buildings. He went to the door of one and knocked. A man in a greasy, stained white shirt and workman's pants appeared. Aniyah didn't like the surly look he gave her. Niccolo spoke to the man and she waited for their conversation to end. She glanced back down the street and realized she had ventured into the unknown with a stranger. It wasn't smart. No matter how cute and charming Niccolo was.

Niccolo accepted keys from the man, who went back in the building, shutting the door.

"Everything okay?" she asked.

"Yes. You ready?" he asked.

"For what?"

Niccolo pointed behind her. She glanced back and saw a yellow Vespa parked against the wall of the building.

"We're going to ride it? Back to the hotel?" she asked.

"Unless you prefer to walk?" he asked.

It was cold. Very nippy close to the sea. She preferred the comfort of a car. Still the idea of traveling by Vespa at night excited her.

"Looks like fun," she said. She'd never ridden a Vespa before but had always wanted to. They walked over and he unlatched the backseat to pass her a helmet. She fastened it on her head. She winced at the sweaty, musky smell it held. She would definitely have to wash her hair when she returned to the hotel. He got on first. She walked up behind the motorbike and then straddled the backseat.

"Do I have to wear this helmet? It will mess up my hair."

He chuckled. "You sound like my wife..."

His voice trailed off as if the memory hurt. He shook his head. "Safety first."

He turned the key on the Vespa and she wrapped her arms around his torso. He felt firm and muscular in her arms. And she loved the deep, woodsy aroma of his aftershave. He sped off and she yelped. She rested her chin on his shoulder and closed her eyes. She thought he was going too fast. They glided along the narrow streets and around one building and then another.

After several tense minutes of fright, Aniyah opened her eyes. Niccolo had complete control of the motorbike. She looked around at the tall buildings they passed and the lovers dining in front of little cafés and shops. It was a very personal tour. They traveled off the promenade back up into the village and arrived at the hotel in under ten minutes. The ride had ended too soon. She was tempted to ask if he could go around the area again. The night was perfect for exploring.

"Here we are," he said.

She eased off and removed the helmet. He accepted it as she tried to smooth down her tangled hair. "That was fun. Ah, thank you—I mean, *grazie*, Niccolo for the jacket." She shrugged it off and handed it over.

He stared at her. There was no mistaking the look he gave her. The man was flirting. She started off and glanced back to see him follow.

"I will walk you to your door."

There were many people inside. Some guests were arriving late. Aniyah noticed his aunt, who was busy speaking with a couple had stopped talking to stare. There was a keen look of disapproval on her face. Niccolo didn't seem to care.

"It is pretty, that charm on your neck. Pearls?" he asked.

She touched the necklace she made. "Yes, my mother's pearls."

"What was your mother's name?" he asked.

"Annemarie," she told him as they climbed the stairs. "What is your mother's name?" she asked.

"Carmella," he answered.

"That's pretty."

They entered the hall. He glanced to the room opposite hers. A strange look passed over his face. It was fleeting, but she caught it. When they reached the door, she turned and faced him. She hadn't expected him to be so close. And he didn't move out of her space. She liked his height. She thought of him to be taller than most men she'd seen thus far in Italy.

She was a tiny beauty with poufy dark brown curls. Her features, from her small pert nose to her full lips and long-lashed almond-shaped brown eyes, were even more delicate in the dimly lit hall. She stared up at him. Her bold and straightforward talk excited him. Women in his life typically told him what he wanted to hear or smothered him with affection. The only other woman who had offered any challenge was Mya.

"I guess this is good night," she said. "Thanks again."

She rose on her toes to kiss his cheek, but her gesture was off by a fraction of an inch, bringing her mouth to the corner of his. Niccolo wasn't sure what came over him, but it happened with lightning-like speed. His face turned and he kissed her. She gasped and went into his arms, opening her mouth fully to him. He brought an arm around her. Lust was rising up so hard and fast he was unable to keep it down. He felt her body heat against him. And the cushion of her perfect breasts crushed to his chest. Her tongue swirled over his and her hand circled his neck.

What was she doing? She was a married woman! What was *he* doing? Had he lost his mind?

When his hand smoothed over her the mound of her butt cheeks, he was lost. He grabbed them both and squeezed hard.

It must have brought her to her senses. She shoved him off and ran into her room, slamming the door. Stunned, Niccolo stood there with his mouth gaping open. He didn't know how he'd lost control, but he had. He shook his head and tried to focus again. He couldn't. His groin felt like it weighed a ton between his legs. He had just kissed a married woman. He'd completely lost his mind.

Aniyah put her hand to her mouth and kept her back to the door. What had she done? Why had she kissed him? And then she'd run from the man? She opened the door to apologize, but he was gone.

"Jeesh, Aniyah! Are you crazy?" she said and closed the door.

She could still feel the kiss and his touch. She put her hands to her head. She had to stop being so reckless. The last thing she wanted was romance. She was done with that. She was here for her.

She walked over to the bed and sat. She slowly smiled. His name was Niccolo. She liked that name.

Chapter 5

The celebration was in full swing when she stepped off the step. It wasn't quite dark yet, but the lights strung up around the pergolas in a weblike design made everything sparkle.

Aniyah was a coward. All day she had avoided Niccolo. She had stayed in her room sleeping or flipping through television channels. She'd had food brought up and wine, too. And she knew the reason. No matter how charming the night with Niccolo had been, the wounds of her failed love affair wouldn't allow her to accept it. Besides, she was uncomfortable lying. Making excuses over why Denton wasn't there only made the pain of his rejection resurface.

She was a coward, but enough boredom could drive any coward out of hiding. Aniyah stepped out into the gardens. There were far more couples than she had seen yesterday on the tour. Several danced or swayed in their seats to the live band playing an Italian love song. Others stood on the buffet line. There was even a group of couples playing boccie, a game Denton taught her once at a local pub.

Aniyah sucked in a deep breath and ignored them all.

Niccolo shook the martini and poured it slowly into the frosted glass. He glanced up to tell David to fetch more olives when he saw Aniyah. She had appeared from thin air. All day he'd searched the faces of guests, expecting to see her. She had never emerged from her room. He'd even checked to see if her husband had joined her yet. Maybe he'd come to his senses and locked her away to make love to her over and over again—as Niccolo would have, given the chance. But his staff told him she ordered food to be delivered and left outside her door. He was concerned.

He shouldn't have been.

Aniyah looked more beautiful than she had the night before. She wore a yellow halter summery dress with a red shawl and those sexy red shoes. She was a splash of sunshine in the evening. She glanced in his direction. He averted his gaze. Maybe he had been too forward with her. Either way he didn't want to scare her away.

It didn't surprise her to see him. What caught her off guard was how after a day of trying to suppress her attraction to him, the same flutter of excitement she experienced yesterday before he'd kissed her returned to her stomach. What would she say to him? Should she ignore him or act casual, like it never happened? Her inner voice warned her it would be best to retreat. But when his eyes connected with hers, she smiled and walked toward him on pure instinct. Why should she deny herself a friend, a conversation with a man, even a kiss when the man she'd thought she loved had walked away?

"Hi," she said when she reached the bar and sat on a stool.

He glanced up. "What can I get for you?"

"Surprise me," she said.

He went about fixing drinks, barely looking her way again. Left alone on the other end of the bar among kissing newlyweds made the brush-off even more awkward. He eventually made her a drink and presented it on a cocktail napkin with barely a smile. And then he stepped away from the bar so the man he'd hired for the job could resume the bartender role. She watched him as she sipped her wine spritzer. It dawned on her why he would turn off the charm and walk away. The man thought she was married. She glanced at the engagement ring on her finger. She'd only worn it to convince everyone of her life. Now it was a glaring stop sign to the man—any man. For the first time since the wedding was called off, she removed her ring. She put it into the pocket inside her little purse and zipped it. And just like that, another weight was lifted from her heart. Why hadn't she done it sooner? *Damn it.*

Her gaze lifted to Niccolo's once more. He was very charismatic. He stopped at several tables to talk with couples and shake the hands of men who were obviously caught up in the same joyful excitement their wives were.

"Signora," a young man said to her left.

Aniyah looked over and accepted a flyer. There would be several contests tomorrow on Valentine's Day. Plenty to entertain the tourists. However, Mi Amore had entered to win the most coveted prize. The seaside resort-hotel would try to be named Lovers' Paradise. The couples would be treated to the most romantic events and each guest would be invited to participate as the resort hosted themed events. The plan was to identify love in all phases, newlyweds, anniversary couples, and couples in the twilight years of their marriage. He wanted to show how love had no bounds. It sounded cute. But it was definitely not something she was interested in. She sighed. She eased off the bar stool with the assistance of the young man.

"Grazie," she said with a smile.

He bowed and gave her a flower.

"Oh, this is sweet." She inhaled the fragrance from the pink petals. She glanced in the direction of Niccolo. He was staring. She was the first to turn her gaze away. The band now serenaded the couples. Most were out of their seats in each other's arms. It was the perfect time to leave.

Niccolo looked up. Aniyah was the loneliest-looking newlywed he'd ever seen. She turned and walked away from the party, headed for the gates to the garden that led to town. The sun had descended and darkness arrived sooner than even he anticipated.

"How is everything, Niccolo?" his aunt asked from behind him.

"Can you watch over things? I need to, ah, see to something," Niccolo said.

His aunt objected, but he left her to the hosting and hurried after Aniyah. When he walked out of the garden to the street, he had lost sight of her. But Niccolo had an idea where she was headed.

The streets overflowed with excitement. Last night her stroll with Niccolo had been calm and relatively uneventful. Tonight it was as if the floodgates had opened and every person had decided to explore the city at the same time. And soon she knew why. It was the day before

Valentine's Day. Musicians would march in the streets until sunrise.

"Excuse me, pardon me. Oh, sorry," she repeated over and over as she pushed her way through the crowd.

"Headed to the town square?" a man who protectively wrapped his arm around his wife's shoulders asked. He spoke English with what she thought might be a German accent. They, too, were being pushed and shoved in the crowds.

"Ah, I guess," she shouted over the cheering and laughter.

"Follow us—we know a better way."

Aniyah kept her eyes on the couple and followed them out of the narrow, sloping street to another. She was forced to walk on her toes in her heels. Why did she even bother with her best shoes for a walk like this?

"This way to the promenade. We can circle back. Are you alone?" he asked.

"I, well, I guess I am…"

"Good, you can come with us," his wife chirped merrily. She looked a bit pink in the face. As if she'd started the drinking early. It was clear that her husband wasn't just protecting her but he was keeping her upright to help her walk.

"I'm Greco, and this here is Margie. We are from Brussels."

"Hi, I'm Aniyah, from Chicago, in the United States," she said.

"Nice to meet you, Aniyah. Those are some pretty fancy shoes," Greco remarked.

"Yeah. Too fancy." She grimaced.

They chuckled.

"We come to Camogli every year at this time. We've been married sixteen years so far."

"Oh, that's sweet. This is the most romantic place in the world. I never knew of this place before…well, I'm glad I came," she said.

Greco pointed out some of the best places to eat during her stay. And shared the history of the village. But his accent was heavy when he spoke fast, and she didn't understand most of it. She just nodded and smiled. Before she realized her destination was so close, she reached it. The center of the village was the heart of the festival. A live band played with a beautiful fountain behind them. People danced and laughed merrily.

"How about a drink!" Margie slurred.

Her husband spun her around happily. He didn't seem to mind that she was inebriated. Aniyah could see how deeply they were in love, even after sixteen years. The couple waved to her to follow, but she gestured that they should go on without her. Drinking was never her thing.

She then took in the wonderful scene before her. Suddenly she didn't feel like an outsider. How could she, among so many pleasant, smiling faces? She walked toward the celebration, this time without the care that had surrounded her before. The heel of her shoe got wedged between two cobblestones. Aniyah gasped and struggled to regain her balance. Thankfully a stranger came to her aid. His hand captured her elbow in time to keep her from falling flat on the ground.

"Careful, *cara*," he said.

She looked over into the smoldering eyes of Niccolo. He smiled and let her go the moment she was able to stand on her own, and when she did she couldn't help but touch his shoulder in thanks.

"What are you doing here?" she asked.

"Same as you, I came for the festival." He nodded to the celebration. She turned her gaze back to the crowd.

"But the party at your hotel?" she asked.

"It goes on until sunrise. Besides, this is my favorite band."

She sensed he was lying. He had come after her, and she was glad he had.

"Those shoes are not made for a walk through Camogli." He smiled down at her feet.

"I know. I didn't plan to come this far. Guess I might need another ride back to the hotel," she chuckled.

He slipped his hand into hers. Surprised, she pulled away. He stared into her eyes. He extended his hand again, and this time she accepted it.

"Come with me," he said. He walked her over to a shopkeeper and scanned the items on display. He then reached into his pocket and removed a few coins. He gave them to the toothless old man and bought her a pair of thong sandals.

Aniyah giggled. She removed her shoes and put the new ones on. They were a perfect fit. The shopkeeper gave her a plastic bag to keep her heels in.

"How did you know this is what I needed most tonight?" she asked with a sense of relief in her voice.

"Most American women make this mistake. That's why you will see the sandals sold in nearly every store."

"A good investment," she said.

There was loud applause behind them. Aniyah glanced back. A crowd had circled around an elderly couple dancing in each other's arms. The old woman spun out and came back into her husband's embrace. Aniyah laughed and clapped.

"They are really into it," she said.

"Of course. We are celebrating St. Valentine," he replied.

"Saint? A real saint, like, biblical?" she asked.

He glanced down to her. "Valentine's Day began in Italy—you know this, right?"

"I read the brochure...but..."

He chuckled. "You thought it was a lie?"

She shrugged. "Not a lie, just a gimmick, you know, a hook to reel us Americans in."

Niccolo stroked his chin. "Would you like to take another walk with me? I can tell you the history," he said.

The people cheered as if to tell her to go for it. Aniyah looked back to see the real reason for the excitement was that the old couple was kissing. It was so sweet.

Niccolo used his two fingers and whistled loudly. "Bravo!" he said.

She clapped. After applauding the couple, the smile he had worn began to dim. There was something on his face that looked familiar. She knew disappointment. It didn't compare to what he must feel being a widower. She couldn't imagine the pain of living in a place like this after losing someone you loved.

"Hey." She touched his arm. "I want to know about St. Valentine."

"Where is your husband?" he asked.

Taken aback, she froze.

"Why do you no longer wear your wedding ring?" he asked.

"You noticed?" she asked.

"I've noticed everything about you since you arrived," he told her.

"I don't want to talk about him. Does that make you uncomfortable?" she asked.

"No. But yesterday... I kissed you. And... I'm sorry. I am not the kind of man to disregard the vows between a man and wife."

"I kissed you back. I'm a big girl. No need to worry

about me or him. You have been kind. A friend to a lonely girl on holiday. I think it's safe for us to be friends. Right?"

He stared at her as if considering the consequences of being friends with a married woman. She nearly opened her mouth to confess that she wasn't. But something held her back. The only defense she had for the weakness she felt each time he stared into her eyes was the lie she'd told. And it was true—her heart was too wounded to trust her feelings, no matter how new and innocent, for another man.

"Friends?" he said. He offered her his arm.

She accepted. "Friends!"

They walked back up the street and around the corner. To her delight he had returned with the yellow Vespa. The scooter was parked among others.

"Ah, so you don't want to go for a walk. Another drive?" she asked.

"Changed my mind. I think I know the perfect place to show you the love in my village."

"Where's my helmet?" She crossed her arms in defiance.

"We aren't going far. No helmet needed," he said.

She put her purse and bag of shoes in the hatch and then got on behind him. Her arms again wrapped comfortably around his waist. It was this exact contact that had made things between them so tempting before.

This time he drove at a moderate speed. There were too many people on the streets to zip around. She spoke into his ear with her chin resting on his shoulder.

"So…was he a saint?" she asked.

"Yes. And Valentine's Day began eight hundred years before the birth of Christ," he said, loud enough for her to hear. He turned the corner and she had to lean with him.

"Eight hundred?" she gasped.

"It was part of ancient Roman culture when the god of purification and fertility was worshipped on February 15."

"Wow. Why that date?" she asked. "Why not the fourteenth or sixteenth?"

"I think I'm being fooled here. Do you know this story?"

"Sort of, but I like the way you tell it," she whispered in his ear and squeezed her arms tighter around him.

He glanced back at her and she tingled inside to be so close to him. He returned his gaze to the street they drove along.

"The date was chosen because February 15 was the end of the Roman calendar and the beginning of spring," he said. They arrived again on the side street near the promenade, but they went down to what looked like a pier where plenty of sailboats were docked.

"So who was St. Valentine?" she asked.

"The story goes that an emperor believed that single men made better soldiers. The emperor banned marriage for young men who could be fighters in his army. A young priest called Valentine thought that this was wrong. So he defied the emperor and continued to marry young lovers in secret."

"Let me guess—that didn't go over well with the king?" she asked.

"Emperor, and no, it did not. When Valentine was discovered, the emperor imprisoned him and sentenced him to death," he said.

"That's terrible," she said.

Niccolo chuckled. "The story isn't over. While Valentine was in prison waiting to be executed, he became friends with one of the jailers. The guard had a young daughter who couldn't see. What Valentine did for the jailer, some, to this day, believe to be a miracle."

"What did he do?" she asked, so fully enthralled by the tale she barely noticed he had parked at the pier. They were now facing the dark sea and could see many boats with lanterns attached bobbing on the water.

"He restored her sight, and the jailer converted to Christianity. The day before he was to be executed, Valentine wrote a letter to the daughter of the jailer. He wished her and her father good health and good fortune. He signed the letter *Your Valentine*."

"Are you serious?" she yelped. "That didn't happen!"

"It did. Google it." Niccolo smiled.

"I will!" she challenged. She eased off the scooter and he came off next. She pointed at the boats. "What is going on?"

"Night tours. Couples go out on the water with a guide who rows them close to the shore. So they can see that," Niccolo glanced back behind him to the village. Aniyah looked back as well. The village was majestic from the pier. Almost every window was lit. The tower houses were almost taller than the cliffs and mountains behind them. They were packed tightly together, and again she loved the soft pastel colors of each.

She put her hands to her hips. "This is beautiful. It's the most beautiful place on earth right now."

"We aren't done. Come," he said. "When your husband arrives, you can surprise him with this gift I give to you tonight, and I will bring you both back here."

"Back to what? The pier?"

Niccolo pointed to a boat that bobbed in the water. It was a small fisherman's boat fit for no more than four people.

"You want me to get on that thing? At night?" she asked.

"I want to show you what St. Valentine sacrificed his life for," he offered.

She chewed on her bottom lip. She could swim. But the lie between them made the offer a bit odd.

"We Italians treat everyone like family. I promise you, Aniyah, you will be safe with me," he said.

"Okay, okay, since you promised." She chuckled.

Niccolo went to the edge of the pier and pulled the boat in closer with the rope. She watched and waited as he tied the boat closer so they could step on it. She still had her doubts—the thing would probably sink the moment she boarded. He extended his hand. She accepted it and he pulled her closer to him.

"I suggest you trust me tonight. I will do nothing to disrespect you," he said into her ear.

She looked up into his eyes and removed her hand from his. If she'd doubted he flirted with her before, she was certain he was doing so now. He went down and into the boat with ease. It dipped and he swayed, but he stood tall. His hands were extended up for her to join him.

Aniyah hesitated. The wind was a bit stronger near the sea. It blew up the hem of her sundress.

"Come on, I got you," he said.

She wanted to close her eyes but knew she couldn't. She decided to accept his offer and take a leap of faith. A man of his word, he took hold of her and brought her over to the boat by her waist as if she weighed nothing. She gasped when the bottoms of her feet landed flat to the wood surface and held onto him when the boat shook violently as if it would topple over. Niccolo gave a deep, throaty chuckle.

"You're okay, *cara*," he said.

"*Cara?* You've said that to me several times. What does it mean?" she asked and let go of him.

"It means…never mind, it's just a word," he said and sat.

She did the same. He reached back and untied the boat. Then he removed the oars latched to the side of it and began to row them away from the pier. He turned them in the water. His back was to the village. She could see everything. The moon was so bright and huge in the sky it shone over them like a spotlight. The waters were calm. It was a perfect night for sailing.

"I can't believe how magical it all is. I've never seen anything like it," she said.

"This is the Golfo Paradiso. It is the most beautiful stretch of the coast."

"What does it translate to?" she asked.

Aniyah tilted her head and Niccolo witnessed another angle of her beauty. Under the moonlight she looked just like his beloved Mya. The resemblance was so striking he couldn't stop staring. This was what caused him problems last night. Her beauty and his loneliness. He would never kiss another man's wife. Never! But he had. And he wanted to again. He cleared his throat. "It means Paradise Gulf. It's what we call the Italian Riviera."

"That's what this is, paradise. Do you come out here often?" she asked.

"No," he said softly. He watched her as she dropped her head back and closed her eyes. He had to look away when his gaze slid down her throat to her breasts. They heaved and fell with each intake of breath.

"What work do you and your husband do?" he asked. Maybe conversation could ease the painful tightness in his chest. And keep him focused.

"Denton is a chef. I do a little of everything, I suppose," she replied.

"Why did Zia Gabriella think you were a nurse?" he asked.

She laughed. "No. I told them I went to nursing school. I didn't finish it. I hated blood, the sight, smell of it. So I was kicked out of school for fainting."

His brows lifted and his eyes stretched wide.

"Then I went to cosmetology school. I do my own hair." She grinned for him.

He nodded that he liked her hair. Tonight she'd used a flowered barrette to pin up the side of her 'fro. But the rest blew wild and free.

"I dropped out. I decided to be a singer. Got a few jobs, and then I became an actress."

"Wow, you have had a lot of jobs," he said.

She frowned. "I'm not a scatterbrain. I know what I want. It just took me longer than most to decide."

"Oh, I meant no offense. I think it sounds exciting. Are you still acting?" he said as he rowed them away from the other boats.

"No. I…well, Denton and I…we decided I would take a break."

Every time she mentioned her husband, she became sad, angry or aloof. He wanted to press her on the subject but decided not to.

"This is so romantic. Do you bring many women out here?" she asked and chuckled.

He supposed it was a joke, but the question burned at the center of his heart. "I would bring my wife here when we needed to talk. It was special to her."

"How did your wife die?" Aniyah asked.

He didn't answer. He remained focused on rowing.

"Niccolo? Is it that painful to discuss?" Aniyah asked cautiously.

He sighed. He closed his eyes but he couldn't open his mouth to share the story. No matter how much time had passed, the thought of Mya's senseless death would forever haunt him.

"Are you okay?"

He opened his eyes. Aniyah had sat forward and was staring intently at him. Her closeness made the sweet smell of her perfume tickle his nose over the strong aroma of the sea. He preferred her smell. Again he had to wonder about her absent husband.

"How did she die?" she asked with concern.

"She was pregnant. We didn't know. The baby was in her fallopian tube. It ruptured," he said.

"An ectopic pregnancy?" Aniyah asked.

"We got to the hospital too late. She died in my arms," he said. Not once since her death had he spoken of how or why she died. Those in his village knew. But he had escaped. Spending many months in France and then in Spain. Never could he share the story with a stranger.

"I'm sorry, Niccolo. She must have been very special," Aniyah said.

"Grazie," he said. He turned the boat so that they could both look over at the place he had known all his life. "That's the old harbor over there. You see the tower houses, the colors?" he asked.

"Yes," she answered.

"They were painted that way originally for the fishermen. When out to sea it made it easier for them to find their way home. On the second of May, the town celebrates with another festival. We have large fish fries all over the coast. Villagers from Portofino and Santa Margherita all attend. Everyone in Liguria is here. It's where

I met my wife. She had studied in Rome and came to Liguria in search of work at our museum. But they turned her away. She was in need of work. I needed a hostess. It was love at first sight."

"So you and she own Mi Amore?" she asked.

"Just me and my aunt now. Before we married it was the family hotel. Mya turned it into the lovers' paradise it became. Her dream was to make every couple feel as loved as she did. It was just who she was. I've told you about Mya, now what is the story of you and your husband?"

Aniyah looked away at the mention of her husband. As she often did.

"I'm cold." She shivered.

"It gets cooler on the water at night. I'll take you back," he said.

When she thanked him and said nothing more, he felt disappointed. The night should not end on disappointment.

Chapter 6

The party continued. They arrived to find the guests full of wine and dancing in celebration. She watched for a moment, not wanting the night to end. She loved hearing Niccolo's stories. And now knowing the way he had lost his beloved, she felt even more drawn to the man. Maybe one day she would have a love story of her own.

"Good night, Aniyah," he said.

"You're going to bed?" she asked.

"No." He smiled. "I have work to do."

"At this hour?" She checked her watch.

"We've entered the contest. Tomorrow this place has to be paradise. The judging starts at five. Plenty to do."

"Can I help?" she asked. "I didn't tell you, but I also went to interior design school. Only for a few courses. But I'm really good at decorating."

He laughed. "Is there a school you haven't attended?"

"Cooking!" She frowned. "I hate to cook!"

His brows lifted. "Really? Food is the next best thing to sex." Niccolo laughed. "Are you hungry?"

She nodded she was. That easy smile of his spread wider. "Then you're in for a treat."

He took her hand again. It was just natural for him to do so. They didn't go through the open doors that led into the lobby of the resort. Instead he took her down another path. It was darker, the bushes weren't as manicured and a few branches snagged her dress. She hoped it wasn't ruined. Niccolo arrived at a door and unlocked it. He held it open for her. She peeked inside the darkness.

"It's okay. Go in," he said.

She braved the door and walked inside. He came in and closed the door behind her. Complete darkness descended over her eyes.

"Niccolo!" she cried out.

She heard movement behind her and then the lights above her flickered on. Large fluorescent lights as bright as the sun. Blinded, she put her hand to her eyes. She lowered them slowly and looked around. They were in a kitchen. A very homey, small one.

"Welcome to my second home," he said.

"Really?" she asked. *What is it with me and men who like to cook?* She walked around the kitchen and smiled. "Okay, I've seen it," she said with a shrug.

"Have a seat. I will prepare you something quick," he said and went to the sink to wash his hands. She sat down. Denton had done all of the cooking and she had never showed any interest. He'd either deliver a meal to her in bed or call her to the kitchen when he was done. He was very territorial about his kitchen. She rested her face in the side of her hand—bored.

"So you grew up here? In this place?" she asked.

"I did. It wasn't quite like this before. We've added to it over the years."

He began to pull out all the ingredients he would need. He had everything—green and yellow peppers, eggplants, prosciutto, and blocks of cheese. She watched him dice ingredients.

"So your husband is a chef?" he asked. "And he never taught you how to cook?"

"Never wanted to learn," she said.

"But food, it's special when prepared by someone you love," he told her.

"Did your wife love to cook?" she asked.

"We loved to cook and feed each other. Yes," he said. She sighed.

He tossed the diced vegetables into a pan with olive oil. He sautéed them with a bit of salt and pepper for about a minute then moved them from the pan to a platter and drizzled balsamic vinegar over them. He picked up a meat mallet to pound the carpaccio.

"Come closer, let me teach you," he said.

"No," she answered.

"I can teach you and you can prepare dinner for him when he arrives. It would be special for you both if you surprise him—"

"I said no!" she snapped.

Niccolo glanced back at her. His brows lowered with concern. He returned his attention to the meat. "Are you and your husband separated?"

Aniyah put her face in her hands. She was tired of the charade. She was tired of the lies. And most of all she was tired of the comparisons. When Niccolo didn't say anything further, she lifted her face from her hands. "We aren't separated. We never married."

He turned away from the food and stared at her with

concern. She nodded that her confession was true. "A few weeks before the wedding, he called it off. Said he didn't want me."

"I don't understand. Why?"

"You don't understand? What about me!" she shouted. "I was with him for three years. I poured my soul into that relationship. What about me?"

He walked over to her and Aniyah stood up. "I want to go upstairs. To my room. Thanks, but I need to go."

He blocked her from leaving. He lifted her chin with his finger. Her eyes pooled with tears but she could still see his face clearly. "I don't understand what kind of man could turn away from someone as special as you. That is what I mean, *cara*," he said.

He tilted her head with the push of his finger underneath her chin and his mouth drew closer. She closed her eyes and swallowed. An intense longing took over her before his lips connected with hers. When she parted hers to respond to him and raised her arms to his neck to draw him in, his mouth moved away. The soft kiss was delivered to her nose, and then to the dent between her brows as her frown deepened.

"Let's finish our meal together," he said in his deep, accented voice, almost lyrical to her ears.

Aniyah opened her eyes. She blinked up into his with confusion. "I told you. I don't like cooking. Besides, it reminds me of him…"

"Then it's time for you to make different memories. Ones that don't include him. Isn't that why you came here under false pretense? To start again? Am I wrong?"

She smiled. "No, Niccolo. You aren't wrong."

He took her left hand and pulled her away from the island in the kitchen and walked her around to the sink.

He kept his hands over hers as he washed them under warm tap water.

"First we clean your hands," he said.

She nodded.

He turned off the tap, dried her hands and brought her over to the platters he had arranged. His hands left hers and settled firmly on her hips. He pressed his groin into her backside.

"A tiny pinch of salt. A tiny pinch of pepper," he said.

For some strange reason the simple request sent her heart to beating erratically against her chest. She slowly shook salt into her palm. Not much. Just a dash. She pinched the tiny grains between two fingers and then sprinkled them over the carpaccio that was pounded flat on the platter. When she was done, Niccolo took her hand and licked the center of her palm to clear its remnants away. Aniyah's breath caught in her throat. She glanced back behind him. His left brow winged up in response and she returned her gaze to the platter. She shook a sprinkle of pepper into her palm and did the same thing. Niccolo again flicked his tongue at her palm and swiped away the pepper.

The groan deep in his throat was so soft she knew it came naturally. He released her hand. His other slid around her lower tummy, grazing over her pelvis. She didn't move toward the counter. Instead she pressed back against him. His towering presence and hard body felt nice.

"Now, do the other side of the meat," he instructed.

She did.

And he responded the same way.

The lesson was a torturous tease because it went as slowly as a first dance. And she tried not to rush through her excitement. In the three years she was with Denton, she'd never felt such unhurried passion from something like having a man help you prepare food. And she had the nerve to believe she was in love with a Chef.

"Drizzle the meat with aioli and then we will mound the arugula in the center of the carpaccio I have prepared."

She glanced over to the third plate of chilled thin beef covered in clear plastic wrap. She did as he instructed, with him helping her from behind. Instead of two hands they worked as one with four. And all the while he remained so comfortingly close.

"What do we do now?" she asked.

"Tomatoes. Do you like them?" he asked against her ear.

"Yes," she said.

"Let me help you cut them. They must be thick, ripe, just the right size to truly enjoy…no?" His hand closed over hers as she held the knife while he held the tomato. The knife sliced into it and cut several thick slices. She seasoned the tomatoes and they put them on another, smaller platter.

He only stopped her to lick her finger before instructing her further. She put cheese on the tomato as he instructed, drizzled them with balsamic vinegar and added some basil leaves. Then arranged all that they had done on two separate serving plates.

"What is this?" she asked, looking at the variety of food.

"Antipasti," he said. "A little of everything. Now we eat, and I can show you how good life can be through food. Make new memories?"

Before he stepped away, she turned and wrapped her arms around his neck to draw him back in. "I thought you were going to teach me how to cook."

"I told you. It's the appetizer. Just the starter..."

"Then let me give you the meal," she said.

Niccolo stared into her eyes. He didn't pull back. And she expected him to do so. After all, she had lied to him. Deceived him and the hotel. None of it seemed to affect him. He had his own intentions. His mouth came down on top of hers.

She tasted like ambrosia, a sweet and spicy treat. The way her tongue swirled up and greeted his was his undoing. There were many questions he had. Who was she? Why had she deceived him? Why had she come exactly when he needed...someone like her? But all he wanted in that heated moment was the kiss. Desire mixed with lust was rising up so hard and fast in his body, he reached his hand up to her head and gently pulled it back to trail kisses to her neck. It was her breasts he truly wanted to suck. How many times had he caught a glimpse of her nipples peeking through the fabric of her summer dress? Yes. He wanted to suck her breasts and then trail his tongue farther. The urge broke the last of his resistance. But he had to stop. He hadn't wanted any woman this bad since Mya.

Niccolo ended the soft brush of his lips down her throat with a small lick to where her neck and shoulder met. Breathless, he pulled back. He let go of her hair and pressed his forehead to hers.

"Don't stop," she panted.

"We must. I...should."

"No. Don't think. Don't think or question it. We can debate the reasons why it happened later. Please, Niccolo. Just let it happen."

Oh, the things he could show her, do to her, right there against the sink. But sex wasn't what he craved. It was intimacy. And then he looked again into her dark, long-lashed eyes and saw the raw need within her as well. Someone had hurt her. Stomped on her heart and pride. Taken for granted all the things a man should worship in his woman. He was the better guy.

"Not here," he said. And then to her surprise he swept her up in his arms.

Aniyah gasped. She was overwhelmed. Niccolo carried her through the kitchen. She hadn't been swept into a man's arms since her father carried her as a child. She didn't recall much of him. and only had pictures of him to remind her of the memory. Niccolo kicked a door open to reveal a room no bigger than the closet in her apartment, holding only a bed and a small table.

"What is this?"

"My room," he breathed and placed her on the tiny bed.

"Your room? You have a suite upstairs. Same floor as mine," she said and looked around as her eyes adjusted to the darkness.

"That was the room I shared with my wife. I don't go into it. I haven't since I returned."

She watched as he lit the lantern. It was an oil lamp and the shadows it cast danced slowly on the wall. He turned his gaze to her.

"I expect nothing from you, Aniyah. If you don't want to do this then say so," he said.

She touched his chest. "Stop pretending that you don't need this as much as I do."

He smiled. "I'm not pretending, not anymore."

He reached behind her neck and touched the tie to her halter dress. "I want to see your breasts. I've wanted to see them all night."

She let him loosen the knot while her eyes remained

trained on his. The top loosened and the two pieces that kept her breasts covered drifted down. Niccolo's gaze lowered to her breasts and then he touched her. His hands were cold. She felt a shiver of anticipation and surprised excitement spear through her. Aniyah liked the rough, callused touch of his fingers as they massaged her. She liked the way he stared at her breasts with a deep longing to do more. Her soft sighs were submission, and he glanced up to her eyes to see that she too wanted more. She reached to the side of her summer dress. With a slow move she drew down the zipper. The dress opened and slipped from her hips. Now she stood before him in her thong.

"Why not tell me you weren't married?" he asked.

"Why not tell me the reason you call me *cara*?" she asked. "We show people what we want them to see, Niccolo. We tell them what we want them to know. Especially when we are hurt."

"You're even more beautiful than I imagined." He advanced on her and she dropped on the bed. He came down over her and she blinked up at him, ready for what was to come next.

The feel of her soft curves against his body fueled his desires. He went for her lips once more. A distraction while he took the liberty to ease his hand down from her breasts to the delta between her thighs. She parted them for him and he was able to touch her warm wet center. His lips again drew from her mouth and brushed over her chin as he buried the lower part of his face against her throat. Niccolo licked her pulse point with his tongue and felt it beating faster and faster. She was his. And it was the greatest gift he'd received in an eternity.

Niccolo's groin tightened, throbbed and strained behind the zipper of his jeans. He'd forgotten to get undressed. With a deep groan of regret, he withdrew and pulled his shirt over his head. He had to stand to undo his belt. She lay there with her legs parted the way he had positioned her. The black lace thong she wore was so thin it had slipped between the plump folds of her sex. Niccolo lowered his zipper.

Aniyah sat up, braced on her elbows and waited for the unveiling. All he could do was nod to the question in her eyes. He wasn't a braggart. He didn't measure his length. But every woman he'd ever been with had made it clear on many occasions how satisfied they were with his loving. His jeans dropped and he lowered his boxers. She reclined on the pillow and extended her hand. He returned to her, wanting their lovemaking to be verbal.

"Do you like what you see?" he asked.

She nodded. "I do."

He hooked his finger in the band of her thong and began to draw it down. He rolled the thin panty off her thighs. "*Cara*—the word means sweetheart. Are you sweet, Aniyah?"

"I can be," she said and spread her knees.

"I want to know," he told her. His face slipped between the cushions of her soft thighs. He inhaled her scent, the beautiful fragrance of her body's desires. The first touch of his tongue across the lips of her sex caused her to quiver. Above him she squirmed. Her hand went to the back of his head and pressed him closer. He teased her. He wanted to delay the pleasure for them both, savor it as he would his favorite vino. His tongue traced the slick entrance of her opening and plunged into the tight wet channel. And then she unleashed what she had held back from him since the first time he touched her. Her pelvis gyrated and her inner muscles constricted around his tunneling tongue. She whimpered his name and it was music to his ears.

"Nic… Nicco… Niccolo," she breathed through grunts and groans.

He wanted her to release. But not yet. So he drew away. And his gaze fell on those thick and plump dark nipples he'd nearly begged to suck the night he stole a forbidden kiss from her. He eased up her and traced his tongue to the tip and then his mouth covered her areola. He sucked as his pelvis rubbed up and down against the heat between her thighs. She was so soft and warm there. He was desperate to slip inside.

"Now, Niccolo. Now, please!" She grabbed his hair and pulled hard to get him off her nipple and tried to scoot lower so he could be inside her. She was ready.

Niccolo lifted his mouth from her breast and gave her another kiss as he arched his back. He dragged his manhood up off the sheet. The condom was in the pocket in his jeans. She didn't ask why he had it. In a city surrounded by lovers even a widower would keep one nearby. Once his manhood was sheathed she ringed it with her hand. She guided him to her entrance. Braced on his hands, he lifted his belly to look between their bodies to see when their union began. He found her entrance then groaned and flexed his hips as he sank deeply inside her.

"Mmm, so good," he wheezed.

She raised her legs and wrapped them around his hips and he went deeper. Every stroke he gave her was measured and slow.

"Yes! Oh, my, yes!" she said.

At first his strokes began slow and easy, but as the friction of his penis became sweltering hot from the motion, he lost his will for control. She dug her fingernails into his buttocks. He continued driving deep, deeper, deeper, with hard thrusts. Sweat dripped from his brow. His eyes were focused on her, only her. Maybe he was guilty of comparing her to his wife. But in that moment he learned so many differences he was shocked and overwhelmed by how lovely and mysterious a woman she was.

"How do you feel, *cara*?" he asked and settled on top of her. His forehead pressed to hers. Their breaths intermixing. He inserted his hands beneath her ass, cupping her to raise her. "Talk to me, *bella*," he said. Squeezing her ass, he changed the angle of his penetration and this time he knew she felt it deeply.

"Yes!" she cried out.

Niccolo knew how to work his pelvis so the hairs that covered it could tickle her love bud and stimulate. His constant thrusting and the friction over her tiny nub had her scratching at his back.

"Come for me, sweetheart," he said. He pounded hard and fast and the small mattress bounced, with the springs groaning and the headboard smacking the wall.

And then it came. All of it. The release of pleasure, frustration and love. Because in that moment two strangers learned that they could love again and that life does go on.

The ceiling above her had character. Cracks and shadows that shifted with flickering lantern flames. She lay on Niccolo's chest. She liked the sound of his breathing.

"Hungry? There's food, remember?"

"No. We can eat it later. I just want to lie here," she said.

He rubbed her back.

"Then tell me your thoughts," he said.

It sounded more like a suggestion than a command. She closed her eyes and tried to put words to her emotions. "When I was three, my mother and father died in a car crash. I was raised by my aunt."

"I'm so sorry, *cara*. That must have been hard," he said.

"I don't know. Maybe it was. I was just a scared, confused kid. My family is good, though. My aunt is my mother's sister, and she tried to keep her alive for me. Told me stories, kept mementos."

"Like the pearls?" he asked.

She traced her fingers over the pearls attached to her necklace. "Yes. Like my pearls. My aunt has a daughter my age and a husband. I always saw them as my family. But now, I have to wonder," she said.

"What is there to wonder? There is no tie stronger than blood," he said.

"I have to wonder why I never truly felt it was enough. Why it meant so much for Denton to propose and for me to marry him on his terms, any terms. I just had this feeling of wanting something that would forever be mine. Not shared with anyone. Does that make sense?"

"Does it have to make sense to be true?" Niccolo asked.

She chuckled. "I suppose not. I've gone from one job to another. From one relationship to another. Denton was the only lasting relationship I've ever had, and it failed. I'm a mess."

"No, no, *cara*, you aren't." He touched her cheek and traced his finger along her jaw.

Aniyah sat up. She turned and straddled him. She put her hands on either side of his head and braced against the headboard. She leaned in and brushed her lips across his. "I didn't plan for this. I came to Italy to get away from love. And here I am in the most romantic place on earth."

He ran his hands up her back, and she loved the way

the motion felt. She could feel him harden beneath her. She sighed and closed her eyes as she moved front to back in a slow glide to stroke his erection, entice him. And it worked. She dropped her head back as his kisses traveled down the line of her neck to her collarbone. Aniyah gripped his shoulders and rose on her knees. She drew air in between her clenched teeth when he helped guide himself back to her opening and she eased down on his length.

"Too much?" he asked in a teasing voice.

She smiled. "It's how I like it."

"Good, mmm, you are so good, *cara*, I can't have enough." He sucked her left and then her right breast as he tried to keep her to him. He squeezed her left butt cheek and she bounced up and down on him. The long strength of his penis stroked the right spot in her as she continued to move. Rippling spasms of desire spread and spiraled all through her pelvis. Aniyah went weak with emotion as she found herself pushed closer and closer to the edge.

"Let go, let go, sweetheart, I have you," he said.

And she did. She cried out and her back arched, which shoved her chest into him. Hot and fast were the waves of passion radiating through her womb. She rarely climaxed so completely and so soon with any man. Not even Denton. She couldn't believe how completely fulfilled it left her.

Niccolo turned from Aniyah's door. It was hard not to ask her to invite him to explore their passions further. After the gift of body and soul he'd received from her, he didn't want to push things. He pressed his hand to her closed door and then he retreated back downstairs to his room. As he made his way through his hotel in the darkness, he sensed someone. He stopped and glanced around. A shadow near the darkest corner of the lobby moved. The person approached him. He stood there waiting. It could be a guest who needed assistance, but something told him it wasn't.

"Who's there?" he asked.

"What are you doing, Niccolo?" his aunt asked in an angry whisper. "With that woman! I saw you two. She's married!"

"It is none of your business, Zia. Go to bed," he said and started off, but she blocked his way.

"You don't even know her! This is Mya's home. And you come back and disgrace her memory by sleeping with someone else's wife? The first woman to walk through the door."

The remark hit harder than a slap. Niccolo fought but failed to keep his rage from his voice before he spoke. "Who are you to judge me? Mya was my wife! Mine! And I mourned her. She's dead, Zia. Dead! I can see whomever the hell I choose. And if you don't like it, you can pack your bags and go back to Genoa. Do you understand me?"

His aunt put her hand to her mouth and her eyes welled with tears. She shook her head in disgust and stormed off in the opposite direction.

"Zia! Zia, wait! I'm sorry." Niccolo called after her. All his life he showed nothing but respect and care to his aunt. But Mya's death had changed him. Since his return, all he had were angry words. It wasn't the man he wanted to be. He shook his head. He returned to his cramped bedroom still smelling of sex and perfume from his night of passion with Aniyah and slammed the door.

It could be a mistake. All of it. And he knew his heart was too fragile to take another hit. But it was already too late. He liked Aniyah. He wanted more of her.

Chapter 7

Aniyah woke. She stretched a bit before rolling over to her left side under the thin sheet. The morning in Italy came with sounds. Soft chirps of birds, someone talking fast in Italian and the honking horn of a motorbike that must have arrived at the gate. She opened her eyes and the sun blinded her. She sat up and put her hand up to shield the heated glare from her face. When she'd finally returned to her room last night, the night breeze was so nice she slept with the windows open. Now she regretted her decision. The sun's rays poured in from both sides. And the air was frigid. She smiled. Last night was wonderful.

Niccolo was wonderful.

Aniyah stretched again. After making love, he'd walked her to her suite door. She nearly drew him in. And when he didn't push for more, she was a little disappointed. But she respected how much of a gentleman he had remained. After all, she'd only known the man a few days.

The phone beside the bed rang. She frowned. A call to her room seemed odd. She hadn't given anyone the number. She pushed aside the sheer drape that surrounded her canopy bed to answer.

"Hello?"

"Signora Jones?" the woman asked.

"Ah, yes, it's me," she said still uncomfortable using Denton's last name. Besides, Niccolo knew the truth. She could drop the entire charade now.

"Can you please come down to the front desk, signora? The manager needs to see you. *Per favore.*"

"Oh, um, okay. I'll be down in twenty minutes," she said and hung up. Niccolo was the owner. Was he the manager, too? What did he have as a surprise for her next? Aniyah got out of bed and hurried with her shower. She didn't have time to deal with her hair. It had frizzed up something awful from the night of sex and sweating. She groomed it into a ponytail, braided it and pinned the hair into a neat chignon. She put on a dab of makeup and splash of perfume. She stopped to look herself over. The strapless coral-pink summer dress was very flattering to her figure. It even had a split on the left side that reached midthigh. Maybe it was too much considering the season, but she decided to go with it.

When she walked out of her room and down the stairs, the burdens of the past two weeks all seemed to fade away. She felt relaxed and even excited about the prospects of her new friendship. With Niccolo she felt a renewed sense of freedom. The realism of her financial straits had slipped her mind. Instead of focusing on her future as her aunt would've liked, her mind once again slipped into romantic fantasies. She could pursue her acting career or maybe even take up traveling through Italy. The world was hers to enjoy.

At the front desk, a young woman and Niccolo's aunt Gabriella waited. They looked up at her approach and glanced at each other. She found their polite smiles to be forced. Had she done something wrong? Yes, she had. She'd spent the night doing something wrong with Niccolo, and it felt so good.

"You wanted to see me?" she asked.

"*Si*, signora. Ah, your bill has come back declined," the young woman informed her.

"What bill?" she asked.

Gabrielle shoved the paper across the counter. "The credit card company has contacted us. A Mr. Denton Jones has disputed the charges on his account. He claims it to be fraud."

Aniyah's heart dropped. She looked down at the bill—close to three grand—and felt sick. Denton had to have found out that she decided to take the honeymoon. For him to cancel the trip on her was just cruel. Especially after all the money she'd lost on the wedding.

"If you could please call your husband and correct this matter, it would be appreciated." Gabriella put the phone in front of her.

Unable to speak, Aniyah stood there frozen.

Niccolo expected an early delivery. He had eight hours to turn this place around in time for the judging, even though he had little hope that he could pull it off. Without his cousin Elaina to manage the decorating and celebratory events for the evening, he was certain to fail.

Lost in thought, he walked through the lobby with his head bowed. And then he heard his aunt's raised voice. He paused. Aniyah stood there staring at his aunt with a wide-eyed expression of fear. Something was wrong. Had his aunt gone after her because of what she thought she knew about them? Livid, he approached the women.

"Signora, I will need you to make the call now. Or please provide another form of payment. Now!" Gabriella insisted.

"Zia? What is the problem?" Niccolo demanded.

"The problem is her husband has accused us of fraud. The credit card company has rejected payment for her stay."

He looked to Aniyah for an explanation. Her large brown eyes began to well with tears. Confused, he looked to his aunt and employee. He wasn't aware she'd been using her ex-fiancé's credit card. That made no sense since the two were separated.

"I'm sorry. I... I'm so embarrassed," Aniyah said in her softest voice.

"It's okay, we can get it sorted out," Niccolo said.

"No." She shook her head and tears dropped. "We can't."

"Where is your husband? This is a couples' resort. Will he be joining you or not!" Gabriella asked.

"Zia! *Basta!*" Niccolo said. He turned his attention back to Aniyah. She was wiping at her tears. "She's not married."

"She's not?" his aunt gasped. "And you knew? She's a thief. A fraud! She lied and stole this man's credit card."

"No. No. I didn't lie. I... I didn't steal it. We—he, ugh—he paid for it, and then he canceled, so I didn't know."

"I've heard enough," Niccolo said. He grabbed Aniyah's wrist and pulled her with him. He walked her into the back office typically used by the staff. Though he intended to speak to her alone, he turned to find that his aunt had joined them. Out of respect he didn't send her away.

"Aniyah, tell us the truth. What happened here?"

"We will call the *polizia*!" Zia Gabriella interjected. "Do you know what they do to Americans caught committing fraud and theft in our country?"

Aniyah put her face in her hands. She shook her head with shame. She then looked up to them and began, "It's like I told you last night. Denton Jones isn't my husband. He was my fiancé. We were supposed to be married on the eleventh, but he dumped me before the wedding. I was so upset I… I decided to keep the honeymoon. It was prepaid. The credit card company can't claim it's fraud. He's doing this to be evil. I swear to you, I am not a thief."

"I understand," Niccolo smiled to comfort her.

"You should have said this the day you arrived. Instead of making up a story of your husband coming later!" His aunt threw her hands up in disbelief. She began to rant in Italian about crooks coming in and out of the town. "Niccolo!" she barked. "What are you going to do about this?"

"I want to speak to you outside, Zia. Now," Niccolo said.

His aunt shot Aniyah a hard glare and then marched out of the room, slamming the door behind her. He wiped his hand down his face. "Can you cover the bill?" he asked.

Aniyah shook her head no, slowly. "I can't even afford an early flight back home. I don't have much money."

"You came to another country with no money?" He frowned.

"I know it sounds crazy. The things I do sometimes don't make sense. But I needed to escape. I guess once again I didn't think it through."

"No, you didn't," he said. "Wait here. Let me speak with my aunt."

"Niccolo!" she said.

He looked back at her.

"Your aunt is right. I should have come clean the day I arrived. I feel like I deceived you again."

"Wait here." He winked before he left.

When he walked out of the office and closed the door behind him, his aunt went on full attack. She charged at him and pointed angrily at the door behind him. "Get her out of here! Now!"

"No. She made a mistake."

"She's a fraud! It's no mistake. And to make it worse, you knew she was lying. What is going on with you, Niccolo?"

"Where's your forgiveness? I've seen you be kinder to thieves in the market than you are with her. You heard her story. She was jilted by her fiancé. Left at the altar. Yes, I knew she wasn't married. I'd never take a married woman to bed. But you thought me capable of it. Is it her you are mad at or me? For leaving? For coming home and not wanting to grieve again with you? Is that the reason for your anger?"

"Does she know that she looks like she could be Mya's twin? Does she? Have you moved on from grieving your wife, or just replaced Mya with another black woman?"

Niccolo jaw clenched with tension. His aunt had hit her mark. And she knew it. "It's my business. I say she stays, she stays!" he said.

His aunt shook her head in disbelief. "You return home and rip into us about letting people visit here with discounts. Forced poor Elaina into an early delivery…"

"She was nine months pregnant…"

"We didn't hear from you over a year. You abandoned

us, Niccolo. And we thought you had finally come home. If she stays, she pays the full amount! Full price!" His aunt turned and stormed away. Niccolo waited until his temper cooled to return to Aniyah. He found her in the office pacing.

"I will call my family. I can have them wire me money and then I can go. But it may take a day or two for my aunt to send it. Please don't put me out on the street."

"You think after what we shared last night I'd throw you out of here on the street?" he asked.

"What happened last night wasn't planned." She sighed. "Plus, it's the second time I deceived you. Are you saying that doesn't matter?"

"No. It matters more that you were desperate enough to take the risk and come to Italy. I know what heartbreak can make you do." Niccolo didn't even dare explore why he wished to be Aniyah's hero. He knew it was a role he could easily fill. So he stepped up and decided to save her the embarrassment of calling her family.

"What is your real name?" he asked.

"Aniyah Marie Taylor," she confessed.

"Well, Aniyah Marie, my *zia* is right about one thing. I don't let people stay here for free."

"I understand. You expect me to pay you back?"

"No. This isn't a bank and I'm not a lender." He smiled. He took a step toward her. His hand traced from her ear down her jaw and neck to the end of her shoulder. She wrinkled her nose as if confused. He fought hard not to reveal how amused he was.

"What do you want from me, Niccolo?" she asked.

"It's not what I want but what I can do for you," he countered.

"And what is that?"

"Offer you a job," he said.

"What?"

"Do you know what today is?"

"Valentine's Day," she replied.

"This is the most important day of the festival. We have an opportunity to turn this place around for profit," he said. "What I mean to say is I lost my event planner, Elaina. Remember her? You were at the birth of her daughter."

She smiled for him. Niccolo loved how pretty she looked when she smiled. "I need some help. I need all the help I can get."

"What can I do?" she asked.

"You tell me. You're an actress, a nurse, an interior decorator. Are you an event planner, too?"

She laughed and went for him. Her arms wrapped around his neck and her body pushed up against his. His hands went down her back and he gripped her butt.

"I can be anything to anyone—it's one of my talents," she said.

"Mmm." He lifted her. The split in her dress was enough of an opening for her to lock her legs around his waist. "Can you help me turn this into a lovers' paradise?"

"I'm not the best person for the job considering my recent affairs," she said and kissed the side of his neck. His grip on her butt tightened. He put her up against the door. His hand eased under her dress and she lowered her legs so he could drag down her panties. He kept her pinned to the door as he kissed her face and neck.

The moment she kicked her panties off her feet he had gone to the cabinet in his office. He brought out a box of condoms.

"For the guests?" she asked.

"For the guests," he chuckled.

She smiled. He freed himself from his zipper and slipped it on. He returned to her. He helped her lift her lovely legs to his waist, and without warning he pushed forward and sank into her tight heat. She gasped.

"Will you accept the job?"

"I'm not qualified," she moaned.

Intense pleasure shivered all the way to the base of his spine. Niccolo pulled out slowly and thrust up into her once more. Her vagina clenched and tension sang through him. Like a man possessed, he began to deliver several jerking thrusts. He caught one of her knees and pinned it back as far as it could go so she could be fully open to receive him. He kept grooving in and out of her until he was empty and his penis flaccid. He rolled his hips in small swirls and dropped his head back with his eyes closed as he continued to release. He was so damn turned on he wished he could do it again.

When the aftershocks subsided, he realized the uncomfortable position he had pinned her in against the door and released her left leg. He kissed her brow.

"Why come to the most romantic place in the world if you weren't in love with the idea of falling in love? That's what these people want me to sell them—love. And like you, lately I've been no expert on the subject."

She nodded. He let her go and she hiked her dress to her waist. He had a lovely view. "I need to clean up. We can't emerge from this office like…like this," she said and walked to the bathroom in the back. He removed his condom and wrapped it in a sheet of paper to dispose of it. He heard the water running. He exhaled deeply. He picked up her panties and went into the bathroom as well. She flushed a handful of tissues and accepted her underwear. He watched her slip them on, finding it sexier than watching her undress. He got rid of the condom and stepped to the sink and washed his hands and cleaned up.

"My answer?"

"Do I lose my room? It's really nice," she asked.

"Do you mind if I pay you a visit?" he asked. "Later tonight?"

"Depends. You need to smooth things over with your aunt." He glanced over at her. "I could hear you two arguing. Even with the door closed. I wish I could speak Italian to understand. But I get the picture. She doesn't want to see you hurt. She's much like my aunt."

"I'll handle her. This is my hotel. I make all decisions and she obeys."

"Is that what it's like working for you? You make the decisions and I obey?" she asked.

"Is that a problem?" He turned and looked at her while he dried his hands.

"I'm not sure if it will look good to your staff if they find out I'm sleeping with the boss," she half joked. "Plus, I'm only here for a few more days after tonight. Why upset everyone?"

"If we pull this off tonight, you will be their hero, and mine. Besides, what's your hurry to return home?" he asked.

"Are you serious?" She frowned.

"Don't I look serious to you?" he asked.

She chewed on her bottom lip. Her arms crossed over her lovely breasts. It would be hard to keep his hands off her. She was right. He needed to be mindful of how his employees viewed this little arrangement.

"Deal." She extended her hand to offer a firm handshake.

"That is not our way. When we make deals we don't shake hands." He took her hand and pulled her to him.

"This is our way," he said. He kissed her left cheek. He then kissed her right cheek and looked into her eyes. "Deal."

She pushed up on her toes and captured his mouth in a sweet yet innocent kiss. "*Grazie*, Signor Niccolo."

"Don't thank me yet. We have plenty of work to do. *Andiamo*. Let me introduce you to your team."

Together they left his office. They found several members of the staff had gathered nearby. The word must have spread that they had an American fraud in their midst. She guessed they expected Niccolo would have her arrested or thrown in the street. He stopped in front of them and waited for her to step to his side. The staff exchanged curious glances. His aunt Gabriella watched from behind the reservation desk. No. She *glared* from behind the desk. To Aniyah's surprise, she wasn't glaring at her but at Niccolo. Why would his aunt be so angry over his generosity? Wasn't her anger misplaced?

"Listen up. This is Aniyah Marie Taylor. She will be taking Elaina's place. We have plenty to do. I want you all to make sure she has whatever she needs," Niccolo said.

The staff exchanged confused glances. Aniyah could only stare at them all in silence. What could she say? What should she do?

"You hired her?" his aunt shouted. "You are unbelievable," she said in disgust.

Niccolo ignored her. He turned his gaze to two other women. "Carla and Mary, please take Aniyah with you to decorate the gardens. Tonight the judges visit. Raphael, you and Anthony are to pass out as many of the flyers as you can to invite everyone to the event. Marco, come with me. We have deliveries and the plenty of other things to do."

"Niccolo," Aniyah said, but her voice was too soft among the staff's chatter. The woman he'd called Mary took her arm and pulled her along. She glanced back at him once more, and he nodded as if to encourage her. She decided to trust him and herself. Hell, she had just planned a wedding all by herself. Even though it hadn't happened, her aunt and cousin had been amazed at what she could do with a limited budget.

Aniyah went to the garden and looked around. Mary and Carla were hanging colorful lanterns and hearts. But the box full of lights and ribbons was untouched. She walked over to them and checked what other decorations they had. She found things that could be useful, like ropes and fishing nets.

"I have an idea," she told the women, who were setting up lanterns for each table.

The women exchanged a look and then went back to hanging the lanterns. It was evident they weren't interested in her feedback. But Aniyah was not going to be dismissed. Besides, she felt a deep sense of gratitude toward Niccolo because of the way he trusted her.

"Ahem. I said I have an idea."

"What is your idea?" Mary asked in a dry tone.

"This!" She shook out the fishing net. "You have lights and ornaments in all shapes. I assume you were going to hang them with ribbons on posts and off the ends of tables. Right?"

The women stared at her for a moment. Carla eventually nodded that she was correct.

Aniyah smiled. "How about we use the nets? We can connect them from post to post with these ropes. There and there. And then run the lights through them. And hang the ornaments you have here. We get the men to tie them up for us and…"

The women didn't smile or nod. They stared. Aniyah tried harder. "We want to create love. But we also want to make this place different from all others. We can use the lights to make the nets sparkle. Trust me, this will be pretty. Can we get help?"

"Maybe Anthony and David will help?" Mary asked.

Carla crossed her arms. She looked up at the sky and then back to Aniyah. She slowly smiled. "It might work. Go send for them."

Aniyah nodded. "Fantastic! I think we should move the tables there. We need a dance area. Closer to where the band will be. There is so little room for dancing. Maybe we can have a kissing booth area. For the couples to come and pose. Last night I saw a photographer. He will be back right?"

"*Si*, signora, he will be back."

"Perfect. Oh!" She clasped her hands together. "I have an idea. We need to do a grand gesture. Something oozing with romance. I know! I know!" She walked over to the bar, where a helium tank stood next to six large boxes of uninflated balloons.

"I got it! It's perfect. Niccolo will love it. But we will surprise him. It will be the conclusion to the night. You with me?"

The women smiled and nodded.

Aniyah laughed. She was made for this job, for this place. She couldn't be happier.

Niccolo lifted his shirt off the ironing board. Its silk threads were still warm from the pressing. He eased it on and turned to look for his watch. He had been so busy all day showering was the last task left to do. The guests had to be arriving. In search of his watch he opened his drawers. When he reached the bottom drawer, he found a picture of Mya inside in her wedding dress. It was the only memento he kept with him always. He picked up the silver frame and a jolt of tenderness speared his heart. For the first time since her death, he didn't feel pain when he looked at her sweet smile. Yes, often a sharp stab of bitter regret would hit him when he passed the locked room they'd once shared. But since Aniyah had occupied that floor he felt the pain lessen. He and Mya had had a wonderful life together three three years. Special, from the first day she showed up at his door in search of a job to their wedding day.

He sat on the edge of the bed. He'd spent a year away to clear his head and let go of his pain. He found it ironic that his return home was the closest he'd come to being healed.

Niccolo stood. He set the picture down flat on the dresser, finished dressing and splashed on aftershave. When he arrived in the garden, it was the first time he paused long enough to take it all in. The girls had changed the entire layout. The tables were pushed back and the floor before the band was open for dancing. There was fishnet hanging over the dance floor with paper hearts dangling above. And true to their culture, tokens of their village decorated the tables. There were little fisherman boats made of paper, and heart shaped mementos. The lanterns and lighting gave the place much more luminance. Of course he'd seen them working. They'd all worked so hard. But to see it on display this way really took him by surprise.

"What do you think?" his aunt Gabriella asked from behind him.

"Did she do this?"

"Yes. With the help of Mary and Carla. They pulled

in the boys, too." His aunt crossed her arms. "She's quite the decorator. Like Mya?"

He tensed but held back from showing his aunt her effect on him. "So I take it you don't approve."

"Of this?" she scoffed. "Even Elaina hasn't been this creative. No. I approve of this. What I don't approve of is you. And if your mother and father were alive to see you now. Ask yourself, would they approve?"

To this accusation he turned and looked at his aunt. He was surprised at the level of hostility he saw in her eyes. But he deserved it. What had he done to prove himself? His aunt was such a sweet, caring woman. His return had been a rough fresh start. But he'd been fully engaged in order to make this place a success. After all, he tended to the guests, took a couple on an excursion yesterday morning, and enrolled in the most important competition in the village. Could she not see the change in him?

"What is it that I have done that is so horrible?" he demanded.

"You didn't send her home. Not because you are generous, Niccolo. And not because you are forgiving. You didn't send her home because of who she reminds you of. You even have her walking around here giving orders and arranging things like Mya. It's disrespectful to your wife, to her memory."

"Mya is dead," he said softly. "And no one feels that greater than me. I am not clinging to her memory. I'm moving forward. I didn't invite that woman here. She came, and she needed help. I…"

His aunt shook her head. "You are moving too fast. I see you smiling at her, I see you looking at her. You're smitten."

"You see what you want to see!" he said.

Gabriella lowered her gaze. "I am not to trying to

challenge you, Niccolo, or question you. I only want to protect you. You aren't ready. You just returned home."

"*Basta!* I've heard enough. We are done with this conversation. Instead of arguing I am going to prove to you I have changed. And change starts with her. If you say a word to her about your feelings…"

"I've said all I plan to say," his aunt said sadly. "I am leaving for Genoa. Tonight."

"Zia? You can't go. I need you," Niccolo said. "Tonight is critical to our success. We need you. Give me a chance. One chance to make this right."

"I've made sure the food is prepared. I've made sure the staff has everything. Elaina has left the *ospedale* and is headed home. I'm going to Genoa and I will see to Elaina and her family. They need me more than you." His aunt looked up to his eyes and touched his cheek. "And what if I am wrong, Niccolo? What if this woman coming here is what you need to move on? I can't stay and see it happen. I am not over grieving Mya. I may never be. I won't be the cause of you not moving past your pain. Call me when you need me."

He leaned in and kissed her left cheek and then the right. She hugged him. Then she was gone.

Niccolo rubbed the tension from his brow. He groaned from a place deep in his throat. He wiped his hand down his face. This was no time to argue. He needed everyone to pull together.

And then came a tap on his back. Niccolo's head turned. He glanced behind him.

She was there.

He found her grinning. And the woman she bloomed into for the night was even more beautiful than the one he'd initially met. In celebration of the evening she wore a red mini dress with thin straps that draped her shoulders.

His gaze went south past her tempting cleavage all the way to her strawberry-pink toes in strappy red sandals.

"What do you think?" she asked.

"Huh?" he said and closed his mouth quick to keep back the drool.

"Of what we've done. Do you like it?" she asked.

He glanced to the arriving guests and those dining. The place was magic. He didn't just like it—he was swept up in the feeling. "You did well. It reminds me…it reminds me of better times here."

"When your wife was alive?" she asked. "People keep saying I remind them of her. It's strange."

"You two are different, but what you do here, what you'd done, well, it's how Mya would have wanted it." His voice was hoarse with emotion that he didn't want her to hear. The decorations weren't the biggest change. They made every effort to be festive and welcoming. It was the flair. Only Mya knew how to add the right amount of flair to turn the gardens into an evening paradise. Was it something keen to American women?

"I have a surprise for you." She pointed over to the left, where what looked to be at least four hundred balloons were anchored to a large heart-shaped weight. They were farther back from the party and swaying in the night breeze.

"What's this?" he asked.

"You'll see!" She grinned.

"Niccolo, they are ready for you," Carla said.

Niccolo walked away from Aniyah toward the band that played for the guests. He glanced back and saw her smiling brightly for him. He smiled in return. A microphone was placed in his hand and he turned to the guests who had found their seats or were making their way over to the open bars.

"Felice, San Valentino... Innamorati a Camgoli... Welcome!" he said to everyone, and the guests are all cheered. "Tonight we have so much planned for you. Games, prizes and of course all the things that make Camogli the true beginning of love. So consider yourselves family, my special guests, and enjoy this night for lovers only!"

The guests used their confetti poppers to release a spray of red, pink and white confetti all over the tables.

Aniyah clapped. She looked around at all the smiling faces and clapped harder. She had spent the day learning of the importance of the night to the people in this village and Mi Amore. The music started. Niccolo grabbed her hand and they were the first to the dance floor. The upbeat tempo had them grinding up against each other. And no one cared. The others joined them. Soon not a person was seated. And the drinks flowed. Niccolo held several drawings and gave out prizes that ranged from a free weekend stay to a private tour along the Golfo Paradiso.

She had done her part.

"Signora," Carla said. "It's time."

Aniyah nodded and accepted the mic. She walked over to the band and gave them the signal. They began to play a sweet ballad. "Everyone, can I have your attention?"

The laughing couples turned their attention to her. Niccolo, who was back behind the bar, looked up curiously.

"Hi! I'm Aniyah. We want to thank you again for sharing this special night with us." She glanced to the judges, who she knew would soon be leaving. "We have a wonderful surprise for you. As you see, each couple will receive their own special bouquet of balloons. And on your tables are heart envelopes and pens. Now, what we will do is write our promise to the person we love and then use the clip to attach it to the balloon. We will release it on the beach tonight. Let's get started!"

Niccolo came from around the bar toward her, but she stopped him with her finger. Carla walked over and gave him a pen and envelope. She winked at him and began to sing the most romantic song in the world, "At Last" by Etta James.

The band played and her melody was pitch-perfect. She never took her eyes off him.

To hear her sing in that beautiful voice stunned him. He was rooted to the spot. Her words created a soul-to-soul connection. He felt the lyrics burning into his heart. It was too much. It was too fast. His head began to swim. His heart felt like it ruptured in his chest. He took a step back, and then another, and he kept stepping back until he turned and walked away.

Aniyah saw him leave and swiftly ended the song. She gave the mic to the closest member of the band and went after Niccolo. He wasn't in the lobby or his office. She even checked his room behind the kitchen. And then it dawned on her where he'd go.

She climbed the stairs and went down the hall to the second flight of stairs. There were two rooms on her floor. One of which had belonged to him and his wife. That door, which had been locked since her arrival, was partially open. Aniyah approached it with caution. She pushed it open. The room was larger than hers and preserved in beauty.

She walked inside and saw Niccolo seated on the bed. The drapes of the canopy were pushed back to the bedposts. His head rested in his hands. She glanced around the room. A woman's clothing hung in the closet. A delicate pair of shoes lay near the dresser where she must have left them. Makeup and perfumes covered the vanity. This was their room.

Niccolo didn't look up. But he had to know she was there. The moon cast enough light for her to see his sorrow and grief. She walked over to the dresser near the bed and picked up the wedding photo. Aniyah was stunned.

It wasn't often that she saw a person who looked like her, but this woman could have been a relative. Aniyah hadn't known his wife was black. "Niccolo? This is your wife?" she asked.

He didn't answer.

"She looks like…she looks like me," Aniyah said. "Niccolo?"

He said nothing.

"Is this why your aunt was upset? Why she didn't want me here? Why people stare at me and tell me I remind them of her? Is this why you…and I? Was I her for you?"

He lifted his head from his hands. "No."

"Don't lie to me!" Aniyah said. "Did you use me? To replace her!"

He stood. He looked at her with tears in his eyes. "At first. Yes. When I first saw you, I couldn't believe how much you looked and sounded like her. I thought God was punishing me again. And then… I realized that you're not her. I saw who you are and realized you could never be her."

"So what? That's why you ran up here—to lick your wounds? Because I couldn't live up to her memory! You made me feel like I was special. That what we felt for each other was special. And all the while you were using me!"

"*No!* That's not why I walked away."

"Then why?" Aniyah asked. To her surprise, this revelation hurt more than Denton. She had spent three years with Denton and hadn't been as honest with him in any of that time as she had been with Niccolo. Her aunt said she was foolhardy. For a long time she hadn't understood why. But now she did. She'd thrown her heart at a stranger. Let him in when she felt most vulnerable. And for what? To be an actress in his little game? To be a stand-in for his wife? To once again be second best.

Brokenhearted, she started for the door. Niccolo caught her hand and stopped her. He drew her toward him and she let him. He embraced her.

"I made love to you, not my wife's memory. When you sang for me, when you shared your soul with me, Aniyah, I felt so guilty. Because in that moment I realized I could move on. I could leave her memory behind and make new ones. With another woman. It's your spirit, your fire. It's all you. Don't punish me for being a coward and not telling you about her being a black American woman who may have favored you. The only real thing you have in common with my dead wife is your ability to touch my heart as she did."

He lifted Aniyah's chin. "I'm not perfect. I'm broken. Nothing I've done in close to two years has healed me. Tonight, these past few days with you, they have changed me. Am I lying? Tell me."

She lowered her gaze. "I'm not her. And you can't promise me when you look at me you won't see her. I can't do this, Niccolo. Not again. My aunt says I'm foolish. I rush into everything. I'm an actress because I'm a dreamer and in acting I can live out my dreams. This is my life. Nothing I ever felt this deeply has paid off for me in the past. Why would it now?"

She shoved him away and escaped to her room. She

closed the door and slumped down against it to the floor. She locked her arms around her knees. Niccolo knocked several times. She ignored him. She heard him walk away. Aniyah cried. She felt like a fool.

Chapter 8

Aniyah heard a tapping sound. She opened her eyes. She had fallen asleep in her dress and shoes. Her makeup was smeared over the pillow. Not since the breakup with Denton had she cried herself to sleep. She was tired of the waste of emotion. She sat up and glanced over to the window. The soft tapping came again. Aniyah glanced at the digital clock. It was after four in the morning. Confused, she scooted off the bed and went to the window. She opened the shutters. When she looked down, she saw Niccolo. He stood underneath her window with a guitar strapped around him.

It took a few tugs, but Aniyah opened the window and leaned out. "What do you want from me?"

"Forgiveness," he said. He strummed the guitar.

"No. It's over, Niccolo…"

"'At last…'" he began. Aniyah couldn't believe how beautiful his voice was. She was frozen. She stood there staring down at him with amazement. He strummed the guitar again and again as he delivered every melodic word of the song with such feeling and sincerity, tears of relief dropped from her eyes. Never in her life had anyone showed her that much love. Something that was all her own.

When he finished, she smiled.

"Let me in," he said.

"I don't know if I can trust you. I don't want to be hurt, Niccolo."

"Me, either. It's a risk. Take it with me," he said.

She stared down at him for a moment, unsure what to do with her vulnerability. Should she protect herself or be brave enough to trust him?

"Let me in," he said again.

She drew the window down. It only took a few minutes for him to arrive. She opened the door and he walked in and closed it. He removed his guitar and took her face into his hands.

"Let me in," he said.

With his mouth only an inch from hers, he said the words to unlock her heart. "I will fight for this. Whatever it is we have. To me it feels like love. I don't care if I've known you for three minutes or three days. I know what love feels like. I'm lucky enough to have experienced it once before in my life."

"This is crazy," she panted.

"No. It's fate. It's destiny. Trust me. Let me love you. I swear it will be only you, *cara.* I can show you what true love feels like."

He swept her up in his arms and carried her to the bed. He pulled down the top of her dress to her waist. He stroked lips, tongue and fingers down her neck to the tops of her breasts. His mouth sucked gently and laved the tip. She pushed his head down farther. She wanted his kisses to go south. And they did. He pushed the material of her dress from her thighs and set aside her panties with his tongue, circling over and over. She dug her hand into his scalp and pushed his head there as she gyrated her pelvis up and down in motion with his devilish licks. And soon she felt herself explode.

In as much time as he took to get her to the breaking point, he found the opportunity to do away with his pants. He was in her with a single thrust. She gripped his shoulders hard. Her eyes stretched wide and she stared into his. He began to glide in and out of her with slow, measured strokes at first, but her movements beneath him hurried his pace. He dropped on her and went desperately fast with his rushed breath gushing over her face. He eased his hands underneath her butt cheeks and squeezed. Together they capitulated and she cried out to the ceiling her pleasure and torment. To be in love with a man again was scary. To be in a strange country with a man she'd never envisioned as her soul mate was even more terrifying. But when he lifted his face and she was able to look deeply into his brown eyes, she believed him. She believed in love again. And that was the biggest surprise.

"Afternoon," Niccolo said.

"Huh?" Aniyah turned over and looked into his eyes. He smiled and kissed her nose. "It's morning."

"No, *cara*, you've been asleep for quite some time. It's almost noon," he said.

Aniyah chuckled. She was wrapped in his arms. Her body tangled with his. She tried to scoot away in modesty, but he wouldn't let her go.

"How did you sleep?" he asked.

"I don't know…better than I thought I would."

He touched her face and her hair. "Stay with me."

"I said I would," she answered.

"No. Stay here. Stay in Camogli. Stay with me," he said.

"Niccolo. We are going too fast. What if—"

He kissed her.

"Don't answer with your brain. Answer with your heart. Stay with me," he said. "You are fearless, Aniyah. You don't run from life, you run *to* it. You think all your decisions are impulsive, and maybe some of them have been. But to me each choice, each disappointment, each mistake brought you here. And I don't want you to have any regrets."

She scooted in close to him. "Is it possible that we did find love, Niccolo? Is it possible that this is where I'm supposed to be?"

"Anything is possible, *cara*," he said and held her.

"What about the hotel? The judges? Did we win?"

"I don't know," he said and stroked her hair.

"What about your aunt? She thinks I'm just a replacement for your dead wife," she reminded him.

"I don't care."

Aniyah closed her eyes. She did what he said. She shut off her brain. She searched deep in her heart for the answer. And it wasn't hard to find. She smiled. "Yes. Yes! I'll stay!"

Niccolo howled. He flipped her over and tickled her. She laughed. There was a knock on the door. They stopped wrestling and Niccolo looked up.

"Niccolo! It's important!" a member of the staff said.

He let her go. Aniyah pulled the sheet up to cover her nakedness. Niccolo put on his shorts and went to the door. He opened it. The young man handed over an envelope.

Niccolo opened it and searched the contents. He pulled out what looked like a certificate. His eyes stretched.

"What? What is it?"

"A fresh start," he said.

"I don't understand?" she asked.

"We did it. We won the contest. We can save this place!"

Aniyah put her hand to her mouth in shock. "We did it?"

Niccolo threw the certificate up in the air. He then dived on the bed. She bounced on the mattress and laughed. He dragged her underneath him. "Aniyah Marie Taylor, I am falling in love with you."

She smiled. "Niccolo, I think I've already fallen in love with you."

He kissed her and she let go. It felt so good.

* * * * *

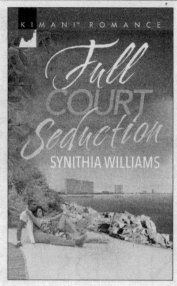

She's all he ever wanted

SHIRLEY HAILSTOCK

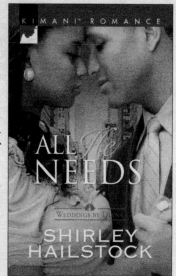

ALL *He* NEEDS

Wedding consultant Renee Hart is finally ready to take the plunge… as creator of an innovative bridal magazine. Newly relocated to the Big Apple, Renee discovers that her former lover is her greatest rival. Now all Carter Hampshire wants is a second chance at forever with her…

Available February 2017!

"This story depicts a nearly perfect evolution from attraction to love!"
—*RT Book Reviews* on *NINE MONTHS WITH THOMAS*

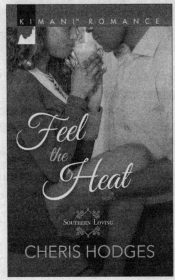

Turn your love of reading into rewards you'll love with

Harlequin My Rewards

**Join for FREE today at
www.HarlequinMyRewards.com**

Earn **FREE BOOKS** of your choice.

Experience **EXCLUSIVE OFFERS** and contests.

Enjoy **BOOK RECOMMENDATIONS**
selected just for you.

PLUS! Sign up now
and get **500** points
right away!

Earn
FREE
REWARDS
Join
Today!
HarlequinMyRewards.com

MYR16R

JUST CAN'T GET ENOUGH?

Join our social communities
and talk to us online.

You will have access to the latest
news on upcoming titles and special
promotions, but most importantly,
you can talk to other fans about your
favorite Harlequin reads.

Harlequin.com/Community

Facebook.com/HarlequinBooks

Twitter.com/HarlequinBooks

Pinterest.com/HarlequinBooks

HSOCIAL

"Mr. Westbrook, I'll seat you now." The hostess approached Hot Suit Guy with a menu.

"That's our table, love." The man stood, extending his hand to her.

Her eyes traveled up the sleeve of his expensive suit. *Definitely athletic cut.*

The man was tall, and even more handsome upon closer inspection. Michael Ealy meets Adam Levine handsome.

Her heart beat a little faster and a jolt of electricity traveled the length of her spine. She shuddered inwardly. Handsome and charming, and he damn well knew it.

A man like that is bad news.

She had two kids and a divorce decree to prove it. It would be safer to pass on the invitation. And she intended to, because that was just what she did. She made sensible choices. Played it safe. But the man's expectant grin taunted her. Dared her to venture beyond the cozy cocoon of her safe and predictable life.

He's being a gentleman. Why not let him?

Maya placed her hand in his and let him pull her to her feet. Heat radiated up her arm from the warmth of his hand on hers. His clean scent—like freshly scrubbed man, new leather and sin—was captivating.

Maybe sin didn't have a scent, per se. But if it did, it would smell like him, with his mischievous smile and eyes so dark and intense they caused a flutter in her belly whenever she looked into them.

She tucked her hand into the bend of his elbow as he followed the hostess to their table. Maya concentrated on putting one foot in front of the other. The simple feat required all of her concentration.

"Thank you." The words tumbled from her lips the second the hostess left them alone. "It was kind of you to come to my rescue, but I doubt dinner with a random stranger was your plan for tonight. I'll order something to go from the bar and let you get back to your evening." The inflection at the end of the phrase indicated it was a question. She hadn't intended it to be. The thinking part of her brain clearly wasn't the part of her body in control at the moment.

His dark eyes glinted in the candlelight. "My motives aren't as altruistic as you might imagine. The opportunity to dine with a beautiful woman presented itself, so I seized it. I'd much prefer your company to eating alone."

Don't miss PLAYING WITH DESIRE
by Reese Ryan, available March 2017
wherever Harlequin® Kimani Romance™
books and ebooks are sold.

KPEXP0217